the Criteria

Kami Westhoff

To my mother, who countered trauma and heartache with love,
light, and laughter.

Acknowledgements

What We Leave Behind	*Redivider*
Until We Surface	*Heavy Feather Review*
The Reliever	*West Branch*
The Criteria	*Reunion: The Dallas Review*
The Fifth Pull	*Passages North*
What the Earth Offers	*Barnstorm Review*
The Concrete Underneath	*Sundog Lit*
Ruby's List	*Jeopardy Magazine*
The Worse You Feel the Better	*Lost Coast Review*
What the Blood Tells You to B	*The Pinch*
Runaway Boy	*New South Review*
The Intakes	*Eclectica*
The Forgetting	*A-Minor Review*
What the Lonely Know	*Permafrost*
Brine and Bone	*Waxwing*

Stories

the
Criteria

What We Leave Behind

By the time they reach us, the damage has been done. The van, upholstered a shade too subtle to name, smells of iron and earth. We hold our hands out to each woman, and they grasp with low tide hands. They always leave something behind: fluids smear the plastic-covered seats, bits of what is meant for the inside the body stick to the seats when the women stand. What they leave depends on so many things: how, when, where. We aren't gods—we only know our own whys. They rise from their seats slowly, as if to avoid the bloody rush to the head that nourishes neurons. Sharpens memory. Though we lead them to the van's stairs, they must descend alone—there isn't room for assistance. Some descend cautiously, hands gripping the railing; some twist laterally, eyes dragging behind; and others, free-handed, sure-footed, face-first.

When the van has emptied, we find our assigned women. The ratio is one of us to three of them, but this is only a formality—all of the women are ours. We palm their shoulders, tell them we are glad they are here. We close in on them, our lips flutter at the curve of their ears. *We know what you did*, we say. *We understand.* And though their mouths flatline, the muscles strapped to blades of their shoulders relax.

We show the women to their rooms. We've painted their names on their doors in shades of purple, but use the simplest of fonts and resisted stripes, flowers, or the polka dots we've heard are now popular. They each have their own room, furnished with just the basics: bed, chair, end table, lamp. Once they've moved in, we do not enter their rooms; what they choose to do inside isn't our concern.

After they've been shown to their rooms, we retreat to the solarium. It may seem we have not yet done much, but this welcoming always raws us. Each welcoming is like our own, and the emotions that cleaved us then cleave us still. We feel a lack in the core of our spines, the base of our brains, the intricate insistence of intestine, parts that are as much us as anything, but we will never see or touch. We are told this room allows the fuel of the sun to reach and recharge us, though the sun is rare at this time of the year. We think too much responsibility might be placed on a sun that can't bring itself to shine for much of the year.

We fold our bodies into poses said to ring toxins from our organs. Or we invert, forcing fluid to fight its way. Some of us find space far from the rest, weave our legs so our soles face the sky, and expand inward.

After an amount of time passes, we regroup. Wine is served, and we feast on chunks of bread, pale and porous to dark and dense. We drink and eat and laugh nervous funeral laughter. We laugh loudly so others hear us and know we are still here. Soon we settle into silence and one of us begins Assessment.

Aurora: asphyxiation. Plastic bags from new pillows, one of us says. It is a common assessment, and warrants no reaction on our part.

Moriah: smoke inhalation, not fire, another says. This another is still able to express hope and bright-sidedness. We raise our wine glasses, lean them into clink against whoever's is close.

Tierra: exposure. More bread has been served, so our mouths are too full for reaction. More wine is served, which makes our assessments lazy.

Ramona: station wagon, lake.

Which make? Which lake? one of us asks as if it matters.

Viola: Toyota, Grand Canyon. We grumble at the repetition, though it has validity.

Katarina: bleach. We groan.

Celeste: shotgun. We imagine.

One of us says it is time to move on, and we sniff at the tired adage. We gulp the wine, shove the bread into the pockets of our robes, link arms, absorb heat from the other. Back in our room, we climb into beds stacked like children's. The walls are brick, the ceiling high. Windows gape at us from above. On intake days, the cool expanse of our sheets is unbearable so we slip into beds already filled with bodies. Our palms, dry as dust, hold breasts like eggs. Our lips part to receive nipples. We draw them taut with the gentle tug of teeth, and suck like mouths are made to do.

In the morning, we prepare a meal for the women: waffles that melt real butter; bacon crisped and light, scones, tiny sausages rolled in pastry dough, fresh berries and whole cream.

They enter the hall and we lead them to the tables broken into *Hows* we've discussed during Assessment. There are fifteen women, and three tables. At first, the women speak only in occasional platitudes: *Excuse me, Yes, please, No thank you.* Eventually, the food in their systems weakens their defenses, and conversation scatters around the room in low tones. We wander the room during their meal, picking up dropped napkins, refilling water, coffee, juice, and milk. We appear to be in servitude, but listen and learn. One woman says her son's birthday is in three days and his gift, an insect explorer's set, sits wrapped in her walk-in closet. Another recites some appointments she will miss: chiropractor, acupuncture, massage; she wonders how we plan to address needs such as spinal alignment and lactic acid festering in muscles. Another shares the split times of her last half-marathon, the tendons in her throat flare with each mile's time.

After breakfast, the women are led to the saltwater pools. They've been given the standard black one-piece suit, black swim cap, and goggles. We watch them descend into the body temperature water, taking note of the speed and fluidity of their entrance. Some aureole the pool, their bodies slick and cautious as seals. Others lean back into the buoyancy, offering their faces to the sky. A few glide through the water with purpose—arms split the surface, legs, locked at the knee, propel. Their mouths take long, calm breaths every four strokes. These ones will be easier— the oxygen of exercise has breathed the body aware, their bodies will welcome us, and what we will leave behind.

We enter the water in suits identical to theirs but wear egg-yolk swim caps. We aren't supposed to swim laps—the comfort of rhythmic breathing and movement distracts us from our observations—but we can dive, press our palms to the porous floor of the pools, toss rings to collect, close our eyes and grope at each other until we're free. Sometimes a few of us synchronize; we spin, lift, lower, and will our underwater parts into impossible positions so the us that is surfaced impresses.

The women eventually drift into the familiarity of their morning groups. Together, their bodies pock the water in inexact constellations. They speak more quietly in the pool, so it is difficult to hear their conversations, but we watch their mouths split, gape, contort, close. We learn from the way their mouths tolerate the motion of words more than the language the words create. The face so often betrays the mouth, as the mind's inclinations do the will of the body.

The pressure of the water mostly resists their body's urge to dispel, but some of us will stay after they've exited the pool to collect what could not be resisted. It is not as unpleasant as it might seem—the body is wise with what it lets go. There is no blood, just blobs of shiny color. We aren't doctors, but if we had to guess, some lose bits of organ, some bone, some muscle and parts we can't begin to name.

Some of us have been here long enough to not remember a before. These new women are of an age that could be our daughters', granddaughters', and so on. Some of us remember our children. Sometimes a new arrival reminds us of our daughters, and we are moved to wonder what they are like now. We laugh at our unlikely guesses—the what-do-you-want-to-be-when-you-grow-up dreams of children: cowgirl astronaut; superhero ninja policeman; president-princess of the world. These are what we remember of them, plausible to us as anything.

After the pools, we escort them to Window Room. As it suggests, it is more glass than brick. Its windows reach from floor to ceiling. Right outside the windows, the perpetual presence of bamboo hisses at the wind. Each woman has a chair, a notebook, and a pen. We welcome each one as she enters the room—envelope her hand with ours, say *This is a safe place for the truth.*

The women's cheeks are pinch-pink from the swim, noses and foreheads shiny. Their skin exhales the scent of chlorine.

One of us begins the session anecdotally: not our stories, of course, but those of women from another time. The details are horrific—the hiss of a blue flame on skin; the thwack of steel meeting bone; the slow fill of lungs with soil, gas, water. We watch the women's faces. The grooves on their foreheads surface, their mouths horizon. After one of us finishes, only seconds pass before hands raise in quick succession. They speak slowly, but without hesitation. The details are often irrelevant: a neighbor mowed his lawn; a sister had called after her first acupuncture appointment; one threw out a pint of creamer that had spoiled. They go on about the size of neighbor's lot, the new lawnmower, a sister that had suffered migraines, the cream flavored with hazelnut.

We move like minutes around the group. Offer room-temperature water, lemon slices straddle the edge of the glasses. Sometimes a woman will place her hand on the knee or shoulder of another. Sometimes a hand receives another, but that kind of intimacy is less common. We learned early on the palm is as sacred as any part. It reveals much through its temperature, texture, the lines that carve or curve, intersect or diverge. They nod, lean in, hmm... at these details, sometimes asking for further clarification. When the speaker finally gets to the killing, it lacks specificity. Sensory detail. There is no dramatic reveal. No tears. No blame is placed, no justification offered. As expected, all speak.

After the session, the women have the afternoon free, while we meet again to decide on the first round. We are silent on the walk back to the solarium. Our heads throb, our throats are bright with blood. We feel as if we've been boiled. Though we are considered more wise, intuitive, gifted with abilities for reason and empathy, we didn't live long enough to suffer of the loss of our children, and cannot fully understand these women. We understand terror. Rage. Psychosis. Delusion, but not the inclination to continue living knowing what we've done.

One of us shouts and points. A man is pacing at the fence, so we go to the gate. We can't help but be drawn to suffering. He tries to force his face between the slats—the pressure flattens the split of his mouth. Skin swells like a thundercloud under his eyes. His body is bent piggy-back, wearing clothes far too warm for the weather. His suffering once would've moved us. We once would've felt it like a fist to the throat, pulled his head to our chest and said, *I'm so sorry. A parent should never outlive their child.* But suffering is tiresome. Distracting. Irrelevant, really. He demands to see his wife, to which we say it is not allowed. He kicks the gate then holds his foot and falls to the ground. We wait until he fits himself into exhaustion. He stands, breathes in slow deep breaths. He slaps at his pants, dust storms and settles. As he retreats, he threatens to kill us all. If only, we think.

We can't remember the last time a man came to the gates. One of us says it has happened before, but has no memory of it. We are quiet for a bit, blink our eyes against the dirt he kicks our way. We entertain the possibility of his promise, shudder from its zap.

Because of this distraction, we have little time to decide which woman will be first. We quickly discuss their willingness to submerge in the pools, the way the water lifted their bodies and let them float. We discuss their stories, how they prepared, the details they used to describe the after. One of us suggests *Tierra*, and another *Moriah*. Usually, we would spend hours in debate, but today we agree upon Tierra and scatter to prepare.

The room's preparations and our procedures may be irrelevant to the success of impregnation, but it gives us something to plan for, makes us feel like we all have a role in this thing. Though it is usually a time when anticipation zips in our blood and we chat only about the light-hearted—new routine to try in the pool; have-you-ever games though we can't remember our nevers; the man's threats linger like listeria in our stomachs. Without words, we haul blocks of ice into the conception room; one of us was an artist, and she creates a forest of Evergreens on the walls. One of us knits a hat and mittens for Tierra; one of us knits two tiny identical sets. The bed is standard, but we cover it with blankets the color of snow. Some of us clip white paper into snowflakes to string from the ceiling, which we've painted the color of winter.

We arrive at Tierra's door after dinner. The women were served wild salmon, spinach and garbanzo bean salad, and ice cream. The air is full of the smell of the sea. Tierra opens the door seconds after our knock. We've chosen well—her face is flushed, her skin is more smooth than speckled, and exhales a buttery scent. We are good at what we do—we don't need to press the backs of our hands to her forehead to know her temperature is slightly above normal, or press our fingers into her body to find the egg-white consistency of ovulation.

Some of the women open their doors to our knock—they watch us pass by as if they aren't watching, still stuck in the belief something only exists if you can see it. They don't yet know where we are taking her, or where we will soon take them, but they all worry their own worst.

We lead her to the room. We open the door and step into the chill. The hesitation of her movement in the hall is gone. She disrobes, though we don't ask her to, and slips into the maw of the covers. The sample sits on the bedside table. Some of us take her hands in ours; some of us kiss her mouth, neck, shoulders. Some of us navigate the soles of her feet with our fingertips. Some of us kiss her breasts and when the nipples stiffen, taste them with our tongues. Some of us pull her legs apart, rest the backs of her knees in the bends of our elbows. Our tongue parts the folds and finds her clitoris, it swells beneath our flutter. We do this until she releases our hands and reaches for our breasts, tugs our tongues into her mouth, raises her hips toward the taste of her in our mouth. Injecting the sample appears an afterthought, but it is all we're here to do.

We lay with her for hours afterward. She talks about her children, about how brave they were, how much the older loved the younger. She tells us about that day she left them. How he led his sister miles before sitting down, leaning against a tree. He pressed his sister against his chest and zipped their bodies together in his sweatshirt. She imagines he sang to his sister until she fell asleep, then closed his eyes and froze to death.

When we lead her back to her room, her steps are like *Shhhs*. There are no other women in the halls. At her door, we thank her, and ask if one of us can spend the night in her room, though her answer is of no concern. We've learned for some women this night is one of the most difficult who already feel the explosion of life in their wombs, or are soon to suffer its bloody rejection.

We retreat to our room. We stay in our own beds that night, the buzz on our tongues, lips, and fingertips strong enough we find pleasure in our own bodies. The rain is so loud we at first think his voice is part of our dreams. One of us stands on a bed and looks out the window. The man from before is again at the gate. Though it is too far and our senses aren't what they once were, his desperation saturates the air like bleach. We put on our robes and shoes and descend the stairs to the gate.

You can't keep her from me, he shouts. Spit strings his mouth together and drips from his chin. He points a gun at us, tries to steady it with his other wrist. His shaking threatens convulsion.

I need to see her.

Which one is yours? One of us asks as if we can't tell.

Mine, he says. He stills, as the rain does. We might say later, *He stilled the rain.*

There is nothing of yours here, one of us says. *Go away.*

He grips the gate's bar. His mouth splits open, teeth, slick with spit, flare.

You really should go, another of us shouts. He remains. Our blood thickens with hormone. Our skin throbs with want. We know he can't leave any more than we can.

If you insist, one of us says. We are wet with the thought.

We open the gate.

We knock him to the ground. We disarm. We press our knees into his shoulders. We sit on his knees, pull down his jeans, wipe the spit from his mouth with our sleeves. We lower our bodies onto his cock. His mouth. The fingers we pry from the clench of his fist. When we are done, our fluids flood his throat and cover his body like the slick of a newborn.

We are electric. He is each of ours—one can't feel another's pleasure any more than their pain. We drag him back through the gate without looking at one another. We will have to talk about it the morning, but for now we retreat to our beds with nothing on our minds but sleep.

Breakfast is late, but the women don't complain. They are so distracted by Tierra's swollen belly they don't notice the steaming bowls of oatmeal we serve. They hover around her; she grins mouth to eyes. Her pupils eclipse the green. She folds her hands over her belly, leans back and adjusts her waistband. The women don't ask *How is this possible?* They refill her cup with decaf, fill her water after each sip.

One of the women asks, *Have you thought of names?* And of course she has.

Do you want a boy or a girl?
One of each.
When are you due?
Any day now.

They quickly plan a baby shower. Moods lifted by the thought of life, even given to those who are destined take it, are a welcome distraction.

Tierra's pregnancy progresses more quickly than usual, so after breakfast we hurry to make arrangements while the women dress for the pools. Tierra will go to a man in his late 40s, who never married but always wanted to. He enjoys kayaking and biking, sleeping late on weekends and sushi, as if any of that matters. We don't want her to be mistreated, but it isn't really any of our business, and what has to happen will happen. We wrap the tiny blue and pink knitted hats and mittens in blue and pink paper.

We go to our room to change into our swimsuits. The night before moistens the crotches of our suits. We can smell the man at the gate on us, more swamp than sea. We collect the women from the hallway, where they've lined up, leaning shoulders and backs against the walls. Tierra's water has broken, so she doesn't swim, but joins the women in line. She has inspired them to share their birth stories: where they were when their water broke, natural or not, how long it took for their infant to latch.

We are almost there when we see him floating on his back. His skin glistens, slick as an oil spill. We feel heat spread across our shoulders and notice the sun is shining. He's the first to have made it this far inside, and we worry about consequences. The desperation from the night before is gone. His body undulates on the surface.

Tierra cries out, and the women lead her to a deckchair, lay their towels over it and fold one into a pillow. They *Shhhh* her, and promise, *Remember, your body is made to do this.* Tierra growls through another contraction. If we were near her, we would encourage her to relax her throat, *Open throat, open cervix.* We want to be by her side, but the man's presence is intolerable. We remind ourselves she'll be fine—here, there are never complications. Mothers never bleed out, babies are never born still or blue or without the instinct to survive.

We dive in eyes open. The water splits and absorbs us. The man's body bobs until the water heals itself. He makes no effort to move. Violence is not our practice, but we imagine our nails ripping back his skin, wonder how deep we'd have to go before skin reveals muscle, muscle to give way to bone.

We swim deeper, and that's when we notice the water is not itself. At first, we think the storm from the night before has scattered debris into the water. We think about how long it will take to coax it into a net and make the water clean again. Then we notice the tiny black eyes, limbless bodies, coiled tails. They scatter when we move, approach when we still. They bump their long snouts against our skin, their touch more imagined than felt. The man sinks until his body rests on the pool's bottom.

They swim in stabs like things never meant for the water, toward the man, who wears the same expression as he did on the surface.

Tierra's scream shatters the water and we remember why it is we are here. What it is we are expected to do. We surface as the second infant slips from her body. Some women can't be trusted with newborns—they can't help who they are. We push them aside and find the infants already latched to her nipples.

It's so much easier this time, she says.

We surround her and let her nurse. There is no harm in the bonding, after all, it never changes anything. We all watch Tierra. We feel the infants' lips on our own nipples, and the cramps contract our uteruses. We, like the other women, feel prickly rush of milk and the warm wet that darkens our suits. We resist, but the women slip out of their suits, their breasts firm and high, milk trickling from their nipples. They weep for relief. One of the women approaches Tierra. Her hands quake toward one of the babies. Tierra slaps it away, hisses a threat. They retreat— they all know what a mother is capable of. They look to one another, the white of their eyes ripe with red. We know they are considering the sharp of each other's teeth on their nipples, the burst of milk into their own mouths. But they crave the smooth of a toothless mouth, the flick of a tiny tongue, thin-lipped clasp and coax.

The man announces his surfacing with a moan. He's covered by a thousand tiny bodies that rest like skin on his body. He is too blissed out to notice the women's approach. When they reach him, they pluck his young from his body, hold their dot mouths to their fat, purple nipples. Some of the women press their feet to the man's face, others hold his arms behind his back. We feel a tug in our throat for the man, a slight sting we calm with a blink.

When the man finally stills, the women rise, their bodies buoyed by the fins of thousands of babies. Their breasts soften with the release of milk, the lids of their eyes lowered against the persistent sun. They sit on the deckchairs, chat quietly about feeding schedules, naptimes, anticipated milestones, expected talents.

We help Tierra stand, supporting her arms with our own. Her children weren't twins before, but it often happens like this. Tierra looks toward the drowned man like she's checking both ways before crossing a street. He might've once belonged to her. None of that matters now. Men are powerless to these women, who are as compelled to be mothers as they are to breathe. Who love their children like every other mother but can't help themselves from ending the lives they've set in motion.

We retreat to the Solarium, bodies low and bent under the weight of gravity. Though we've never seen a day like today, we've learned to resist the inclination to be surprised. We've learned each group of women is different, but here for the same reason, destined to be what they are. What we are.

Until We Surface

The quease in our bellies rises and recedes with the water's insistent motion. We close our eyes, beat back the bile with an onslaught of swallow. For Andrew its worse, of course. He opens the kitchen window and vomits. His mother is a pinprick for now, but her motion snags the sky, tears it into a woman shaped hole. As she rows toward us, the water splits at the oars' insistence. Andrew wretches again, and we feel it burn from belly to brain.

It reminds us of the chalky tang of road trip medicine, so we swallow its memory to ease the nausea. When his mother reaches us, she steps from her boat to our porch and the water heals itself. Her eyes are fat with hope. Andrew closes the window, stomps upstairs. His mother clomps on the steps like a drunk, the sea not yet ready to release her. Her shirt gapes open and shows her breasts. We remember the soft skin of aureole against our newborn lips. We taste her milk surge into our mouths, suck hard until the hind milk relents and coats our tongues.

Andrew, she shouts, already our bellies are full of only echo. She looks at us, pulls her shirt together and tries to button it with water-logged fingers. The shirt falls open again, milk trickles from her nipples. We suffer the sight. We tell ourselves it would only sour our tongues, curdle in our stomachs, but we are stupid with want.

Andrew, please. Andrew screams into the face of his pillow. We are proud of him—one of us showed him this trick after the last time his mother came and he carved canyons into his throat to let the air in. He is getting stronger.

His mother collapses on our porch. When she lifts her head to call his name again, we see the slivers scattered. We hear the upstairs window creak open, vomit splats onto the stairs of the porch. We open the door—she is too weak to make a move. We kick her and she rolls down the stairs. Her head thuds against each: one, two, three, four. We use the oars to unshore her boat, and though one of us wants to keep them, send her off with nothing but the mood of the sea to guide her, we toss them in. She is soon that same pinprick. Andrew finds a place on the couch. Though he will always be six, his hair long ago shocked itself white. We know he was old enough to undo his carseat when he died, but not the safety locks. In case he gets another chance, we showed him the ballpoint pen to the window trick. If you do it just right, we say, the glass will shatter and you might survive.

We lift him light as a feather, stiff as a board. His body is heavy as ten, water-logged and given up. We carry him up the stairs, careful with his head when we turn the corner into the bedroom. We lay him on the bed and tuck him warm. He opens his mouth, gulps at the air, coughs. We tell him how brave he is. We tell him we don't know if we could've resisted. He coughs up something—it is slick and dark and we pretend to not notice.

We hear a scream outside and think it's his mother, but when we look out the window, we see the sky has unstitched itself from the sea. Mountains crag the sky and our breath exposes the air. Our lips blue. We scatter and search—there are drawers everywhere—mittens, hats, scarves, blankets. Ice pricks our tongues, settles heavy on the branches of our lungs like birds. One of us says we should, so we hum to thaw out our throats.

We pause to breathe under the warmth of the blankets, but the tune carries on. The humming spills over us, the scent of it reminds us of Saturday mornings. We move to the window, the blankets shoosh when they hit the floor. The world is a blizzard, and another mother sits crisscross apple sauce on the snow. A somewhere sun glints against her sunglasses. She sees us, waves us near.

Sarah, Nathan, she says. *Do you know them? Are they here?*

We open our mouths, close them around the heat of her words. The ice in our lungs melts and we cough them dry. Sarah and Nathan are here, but we block them from the sight of her.

Be strong, we say. *Take our blankets.*

Our skin reddens, we scratch until our fingernails are filled. We pick them clean and scratch again.

She says, *I'm here to save you.*

We think it might be okay to approach her. What's the harm? We smell the tang of her and feel the press of her fingertips on our bellies, necks, the pits of our arms and knees. Our bodies writhe beneath the fleshy pads of her tickle. We giggle until we choke and the cough is back.

Sarah, Nathan, she repeats. It's not a question this time.

One of us slips in the snow, and the rest of us fall like a joke. One of us throws a snowball-it explodes against her face. We press snow into perfect spheres—our aim is what we would lie it to be. A snowball connects just right, and her nose cracks and scatters blood across the snow. It melts in our mouths before we notice our faces buried in the white. The cold will twinge our teeth for hours, but the warm rust of her blood coats our throat like honey. Calms our cough. We remember the hum of humidifier. The gentle burn of Vicks on our chests. Coughing into the crooks of our elbows. Sick days with juice on the couch, the cool of our mother's wrist against our foreheads. The mother is gone when we are done with the memory. Sarah and Nathan watch from the door. For a minute, we lost ourselves, and they watch us with you-know-better faces.

We put on dry clothes. We talk about where we went wrong, but we know we wouldn't do anything differently. We make hot chocolate, knock on their door.

We are sorry, we say to the door. *We lost ourselves.*

They don't answer. We drink the hot chocolate and sing the song we know Nathan sang to Sarah before they fell asleep in the blizzard waiting for their mother to come back. She'd driven miles by the time their bodies finally relented. We wait at the door in case they forgive us.

When the door opens, we immediately regret our step inside. The room is a tunnel, its walls become ceiling become floor. We are all elbows and knees and shoulders, so some of us press forward into the cool dark. A click startles us, and we spill over one another. Those of us in front are mowed, faces stamped, ribs snapped, one of us ruptures a spleen. We apologize, of course, but press on, knowing the healing will come regardless of being wanted.

One of us shouts, *No! The other way!* We slip our hands under the armpits of the trampled, drag them until they're made again. The tunnel is longer than we first thought. It gives us time to think, to remember what it reminds us of, and then we are in our new swimsuits, chlorine seeping through our skin into memory, throats thick with scream, bellies full of laughter. Waterslides. We still hope. We still live in the forgotten longer than we should. We still expect the pool's surface to split open, let us in, hold us under, rise us until we surface.

We smell something sweet then see her at the end of the tunnel. She is holding waffle cones. Our tongues burrow and ice cream drips onto our shirts before we can say *We're not allowed.*

Mary! The mother says, and we still our tongues. Mary shits herself, the force of it sounds like gunfire. Her mother shows us her empty hands.

See, she says, turns her palms up like we've asked to read them. *You can trust me.*

Mary is still shitting, her mother's hands again hold cones. We smell the sweet on each other's tongues. Chocolate areoles our mouths, the valley between our thumbs and pointers stained dark. We lick the sweet from each other's hands and mouths.

Mary is too weak to walk, so we take turns carrying her on our backs. Her mother follows us, carrying baby wipes, a pair of pink and white leggings, cream to cool the raging rash.

Mary, her mother says. *I only want to help you.*

Mary's diarrhea is more like urine now—it drips in a steady brown from her shoes. One of us notices the foam spilling from her mouth, her eyes are only whites. She died when she was three, so she suffers more with body than mind. Her want of mother is more like thirst, or the urge to gag when a finger is down your throat. She is our favorite. She's so often compelled by happiness—giggles when we lift her above our head, spin her helicopter. We argue over who gets to read her favorite books: *On the Day You Were Born, I Love You Forever, Where the Sidewalk Ends.* She draws pictures of us—huge eyes, arms and legs like spiders, smiles big enough to swallow our heads.

I didn't mean to, her mother says. Suffering has left her mother more bone than body, but that's what you get, isn't it? Mary is convulsing now; things have gone on too long. We

wonder about the length of her mother's tongue. We wonder if
her throat and stomach have rawed and blistered like Mary's. We
wonder ourselves deep, drag our nails against her esophagus, kick
holes in her gut so the acid leaks out. We think, *Now you know
what it feels like.*

The one of us that was carrying Mary calls us off, promises
she's okay. We are quickly with her—she scoops applesauce into
her mouth, nibbles crust-less toast between each bite. We clutch
our bellies and sad our mouths—the ice cream won't work again,
we promise. We are sorry, we say, we wanted.

Mary is back to herself before we wipe the applesauce from
her chin. We know trauma has carved into her mind, tucked
itself away to later affect her in unpredictable ways, but since
none of us age, there isn't a later for her, so we worry simply
about the present, which seems to burst in every direction. We
wonder if our mothers felt this way—the incessant throb of the
present like a sliver under a fingernail.

It isn't always like this. There are times when the mothers leave
us be. We use these times to prepare for the next visit. We read
books on parenting. We play games that encourage logic:
rummy, chess, dominoes. Games that ask us to understand the
motivations of our opponents before our opponents understand
their own. We talk about our fathers, our grandparents, our
siblings who were spared. Though they each failed us, we've
forgiven them. We swear if we saw them again we wouldn't ask
Why didn't you save us?

Our house makes much more sense during these times.
When we take off our tennis shoes in one place they stay there
until we lace them up again. If our foot slips out from under us
on the stairs we land at the bottom. We brush our teeth first and

last thing, floss when the brushing isn't enough. The weather is mild, but we stay inside, for fear of how quickly a sky can tear itself open and let in the storm.

We are coloring when we hear barking. A dog! We imagine our own or the one we always wanted and run to the door. A golden retriever pants on the porch, a stick wedged under its paws. It looks at us, tilts its head and whimpers. We collapse, bury our noses into its fur. It rolls over, trusts us belly up. This could be it, we think. Is it finally over? We jump into the water, hold our palms for the tiny fish to swim into. Our dog, now a black lab, paddles past us toward the stick. We see our friends carving their names into the sand. We swim to shore and scatter. Some of us lift rocks and catch what cowers below. Some build towers of stones.

We hear laughter, deep and measured. Its octave stills us, and we are back in our house, peeking out the front door, water foot-shaped pools at our feet. We gasp and push each other out of the way and gasp again. A father. We've heard this is possible, but never seen one. He sits on the steps of the porch facing away from us. In the sky, birds' wings split the air into something new. Trees have sprouted high and ancient all directions. We remember searching for mushrooms at the base of alders with our fathers. Brushing the leaves away as if they covered something precious. Irreplaceable. We smell the onions hissing in the pan, see the fork of our father lift the mushrooms to our mouths, *Just try one bite...*

He stands, and we are in a tent. We lie flat, zip the sleeping bag to our throats, wiggle deep in its cave. We hear the sounds of a thousand creatures waiting to eat us. We inch our bodies close to the father whose back is toward us. When we are close enough to smell what we know is only his scent, to scuff our cheeks with the stubble on his, his arm reaches back and pulls us tight.

We think we must've fallen asleep, because of the crick in our necks and taste in our mouths. We sit up, but the ceiling is too low, so we lay flat. Some of us smell the hiss of fire and flesh, some of us feel the flames' insistence. We reach for our father, but only find the skin of each other, the temperature and texture of cheese pizza. We reach in the other direction, and flesh gives way to our fingertips like rotten fruit. One of us screams, and the air that presses it forward smells like mushrooms. We think we should move, but we still feel the touch of our father's hand on our backs where he could feel the insistence of our breath, the beat of our heart, the twitch of a just-asleep fall. We stay in his touch for only the tick—we are back on our porch before the tock.

Those of us that didn't have fathers open the door. We are more mush than muscle, more twig than bone, but they are careful to keep us together. They prop us up on couches, bring us things that were once our favorites: Doritos. Red Vines. Root Beer. None of us knows whose father it was—we never saw the face, so each of us claim him as our own. We know his scent, and that scent is the memory we can trust. He belongs to so many of us, we all share—even those that never knew their father— stories about him. We lie. We tell the truth. We retreat into the memory of their touch when the words get too hard to speak. We remember things they never did, forget the things they did. A father. We think this visit must mean something. We wonder if someone isn't being honest about how they got here. We look at each other for the smear of lie on our faces, but of course, all of our faces are smeared with the tragedy of the mother.

Maybe he has come to protect us, one of us says.

Some of us laugh at the idea, others, though not prone to violence against one another, think of the stitching of one lip to another for the utterance. No one here believes any father had a chance.

This break from the mother has weakened us. We lie on the floors, our bodies S's and T's and H's, and wait. Some mothers never come, and though we've all seen the cleaving their visits leave, we wait for them like a last-one-picked-up child. From what we guess, only the mothers that would do it again visit. That we exist, somehow, gnaws at them, keeps them from moving on to wherever it is they should go. We think we suffer most, those with these mothers, but who really knows the slam of ache another feels, or why.

At some point, we dream. We aren't sure we've done this since we've been here. In the dream, we hear light laughter, the tink of glass to glass. Outside, they've spread out blankets on the expanse of a lush lawn. They wear sundresses and sunglasses. Some have hats with brims as wide as their bodies. They show each other photos, drawings, bracelets and necklaces heavy with beads. They lie on their left sides and rub their huge bellies and in the dream we are born.

A scent, irony, musky, thick—like we imagine a body smells on the inside—enters the house. A thrash of wings, caws and squawks and shrieks, sucks the air from the sky. Something smashes all the windows of the house but there is no glass for us to be careful. The quease is back, so we look out, expecting to find the sea, but only see the underneath. We hold hands, piggy-back our littlest, and move toward the stairs. We leave this place often, but never because we mean to. We are cautious on the steps, which crackle like fire with the weight of us. Fish have stopped gasping for air. Seagulls tear into them, crabs feast on the bits left behind. One of us points at the dark mound of a whale in the distance. Jellyfish deflate into unremarkable blobs. Their bodies, like transparent organs, jiggle from the poke of our feet. One of us warns they can sting you, even after they are dead. We wait to feel the slam, slit, surge of a mother. We try to remember something other than the now. Did we have a pet fish? Drop crabs through the sharp mouth of a pop can and shake it to make music? Did a seagull swoop down to steal the bread from our picnic? We crave the taste of nothing. Our lips don't gape for the warmth of a nipple. The hair on our skin doesn't prick with the want of touch. Something must be about to happen, we think. Or something must've happened before this.

We wander among the animals. Press outward into the whatever. We no longer feel the doughy palms of each other, or the pressure of the arm to throat of a piggyback. If someone were to look down upon us, they might say our bodies formed unlikely constellations. Or they might say we shouldn't be down here alone. Or they might say it looks like something might've been there once, and wonder how it ever managed to survive.

Make Things Right

We never said we knew what it was like to be them. To split open like that: blood and muscle and tissue and bone into blood and muscle and tissue and bone. To be consumed from the inside. We watched them collapse into the burst of life in their bellies, washed our hands before we touched them, scrubbed at our bodies in ways we never had. We promised that their swelling bodies still made ours throb, and we meant it. We pressed our lips where the slick heads of our babies would crown. Our mouths ached as their nipples thickened in preparation for the suck. Our bodies fattened, but refused to miracle. We knew we would pay for this. Later, we'd admit the excuses we made as they entered into the unravel. Claim we didn't but we saw it coming. Blame slackens our faces like a stroke. We suffer for ourselves, for the mothers, for the children we wanted to birth so we could say we mattered.

*

We busy ourselves with preparations. We don't know how long the children will be in the house, and we have so much to do to make things right. The house is two-story, second floor windows as wide as a firefighter. We knot a rope every six inches, slip it around the leg of the dresser, coil it near the sill. We take turns escaping, and though the distance between knots is too short for a grown man, we figure it's right for a child. We wonder if they learned the trick of the climb in P.E. We hope they know to use their feet.

The porch is a wrap-around, the height of the stairs short enough to misstep a full grown—the children's bodies will easily learn its language. We hang hammocks so they can cocoon, flip over and see the world upside down if it helps. We plant daisies in flowerboxes. Miniature replicas of the house, stuffed with birdseed, dangle from the rafters. Many infants and toddlers will live here, so we build a gate, slats distanced to code.

We do things we were once asked to do but didn't. Measure and saw wood into trim for the kitchen. We wash the outside of windows, slide a hot rag in the screen door's tracking. We fix the dishwasher, again, and swear at its perpetual failing. We replace knob and tube. Sit slant on the roof and patch it new. We climb a ladder and whack hornets' nests from the awning. Barehanded, we pile the nests in a wheelbarrow, don't bother to swat away the stings. When one of us falls from the ladder, arm bent opposite at the elbow, we huddle around him, desperate for a scrap of suffering. The body heals too quickly here—we don't have the gift of prolonged physical pain.

We help each other out as only fathers who've failed like us can. Even with our efforts, the house is always full of poison. We dump bleach into the drain, scrub the sink with baking soda. One of us remembers the skin of his wife's hands, bright with burn of bleach, peeling off in jagged, transparent strips. *Is that possible,* one of asks, and we laugh without being amused.

We dig a hole and pour in oils we once rubbed onto the backs or chests or feet of our wives when they asked us to, or when we thought they wanted it. The sassafras reminds us of burgers and root beer, our children's lips slippery from French fries. We suffer it. Camphor settles in the twigs of our lungs. We remember singing "John Brown's Baby," and leaving the wrong words out with each verse, pressing the bellies of our wrists to sweaty foreheads. We suffer this, too.

We pour nail polish remover into the fireplace and breathe its hiss into the backs of our lungs. In the haze of its poison, we let ourselves remember Sunday nights after bath. The children's soles, cautious of the tickle, pressed against our palms while we painted nails in every other, added the glitter top coat once it was dry. We look at our own feet—some of us still have a scrape of color from the children's *Your turn, Papa*. We gather around to get a closer look. Don't stare too long or you'll look it away. When we've had enough, we pass around the bottle of mouthwash until it etches its fresh into our throats.

Immediate threats addressed, we move on to the more subtle toxics. We open all the cans of tuna, remembering our signature lunch, tuna salad in giant clam shell pasta. We shove our mouths full even though it's Albacore. What does mercury matter to us? We rip open mac and cheese boxes, whip smooth its egg yolk powder and put in on thick. We find a crinkling paper bag of cherries, swallow them whole. If there were apples, we'd split them in half, pluck the seeds and eat those too. We eat raw almonds, gnaw on cracked open avocado pit, and ground beef days past its *Best by*. We eat until the food threatens our throat with its surge, then we vomit until we taste the bitterness of bile.

Guts emptied, we shuffle to the wrap-around porch for the gathering. We never know when these gatherings will occur, we just find ourselves in them without intention. The fit is tight, there are many of us, but we've long since shrugged the need for privacy, for space. Outside the air is arctic. We've stocked the house with blankets and jackets, hats and Kleenex in case one of the children thinks to wipe the noses of the youngers, who never learned to use their sleeves. We blow air from our lungs like smokers—only when it's this cold do we speak our *Hows*. We fill clouds of breath with the details, each telling worse than the one before and after. Our breath freezes the air before us, hits the ground in a shatter.

Some here never met our children, but with unlimited time to imagine, and borrowed details from the suffering of others, still take a turn. For some reason, these are the stories that sour our tongues, and settle like rot in the hollow. These are the ones that rage us, and we dive into the fight like the winner matters. We go for each other's throat first, to shut our goddamn mouths. We squeeze until blood vessels burst the whites of our eyes red. We smash jaws with fists until they hang loose from their hinges. We grab each other's testicles, squeeze until we feel the pop.

We don't have much time like this, so we still, some of us in piles, some spooned in the arc of others. We burrow into the crotch of our pain, nurse it like a newborn. It reminds us of the soft skin of our mothers' breasts, our infant palms open against the fleshy expanse. It reminds us of nipples, firm and textured on our tongues. It reminds us of the burst of the letdown, of the liquid warmth in our mouths and throats and bellies. We shit ourselves, savor its scent, in it, the tang of our mothers.

The healing is unbearable. Our brains resist, but our bodies can't help but wedge into the warm, moist stench. The sweet prick of the freeze is gone. Our bodies absorb our tears and spit and blood. The ache of the fight more an idea than a memory.

We file down the stairs without caution. Some of us stumble and don't bother grabbing the railing. We breathe more moisture than oxygen, water drips from our pant legs. We move like slow motion. One of us points skyward, and the bright belly of a pigeon (or is it a trout?) passes by with no notice of what's below. We follow the back in front of us to the field where the station wagon is parked. At one time it wasn't parked there, but then it was. Even if you didn't know any of us, you'd know who it belongs to by our approach. We tell him he doesn't have to, that we will take care of it. We say sit, dip your head below your heart, square-breathe to calm your nerves. But of course we know the impossibility of such a suggestion. So ridiculous it's almost a joke.

He turns the engine—it coughs, thick and wet, then quits. We know it spent weeks at the bottom of the lake, child still strapped into its car seat. We say we've heard drowning is a painless death—quick, even, if you just let it happen. We are hopeful the damage to the car is too severe, but here all the wrong things heal. We disconnected the power locks and windows, a safety feature we'd once insisted upon—car-jackers, kidnappers, rapists at red lights—certain that which threatened did so from outside. We test the latch on the carseat, ease its release with WD-40. We read its manual, still wedged between the receipt for new tires and a pass for the parkade. We do the things it says not to do. Loosen straps. Slip a folded towel under the seat so things aren't quite level. We install it in the middle, where there is only a lapbelt, when the *Caution* clearly states a shoulder strap is more secure. We talk about all the other ways to save these ones: life-jackets, hammers, floating devices attached to cushions, but worry the mothers are onto us, and would surely notice anything that offered an out. We scatter pens throughout the car because one of us saw a trick. We do what we can knowing it will never be enough.

One of us lifts the floor mat, and the left-behind cleaves. Crumbled goldfish, the final ridged bite of string cheese. Cheerios. The last licks of a Dum Dum. We throw each other out of the way to get close. We press the crumbs to the tip of our fingers, a taste of something the sticky hand of a lost might've touched. Collect the Os, in their perpetual shock, imagine the playdate or gymnastics class they followed. There is only one sucker—one of us suggests we each have a lick—so we do this. We comfort each other after the hint of sour or sweet or ginger has been swallowed away. Sometimes our suffering is lessened by the suffering of others, so we decide some will have extra licks so the rest can watch the collapse into memory.

We leave the car doors unlocked, *Someone, Please steal the fucker,* one of us says. The language reminds us of the type of men we once thought we were, or thought we should be. We belch. We fart, and don't bother with a joke. Our chests rooster, our voices dip an octave. *Fucking bastard!* One of us says at no one in particular. *Fucking bitch!* Another yells. *Goddamn, motherfucking bitch! Whore!*

We are all chest and voice now, and we walk like our cocks make it hard to. Our spit pelts the ground like gunfire. Deep-snort, throat-thrust, mouth-filling spit. We blow snot from our noses, pinch it off with our fingertips.

Cunt! One of us says. We still. The air full of bull-breath. The word throbs in our veins. *Cunt!* We know we shouldn't, but our mouths bark it out, we taste it on our tongues. *Cunt! Cunt! Cunt!* Our eyes are more black than white. We wait for reprimand, never said this word without it. We look toward the trees that surround us on all sides, squint for signs of life. We rarely see animals here—we long for the distraction of a coyote, or a fawn, bright with spots. The skitter of a squirrel. Or even a skunk. One goddamn skunk. We once saw a bear skulking along the tree line and decided it had to be a mother grizzly. We watched her move, her thick coat rolling over her shoulder blades with each step. She rose onto her hind legs, and we gasped at the sight of her massive belly, teats tugged long by the strength of the suck. We knew her cubs must be close behind, watching her determine which world she wanted them to live in. We felt the cool brown earth on the pads of her paws, the scratch of claw against rock. We smelled our stench through her snout, the guilt-rot in our armpits and crotches. We lifted our shirts and thought *Come get me*, desperate to bury our faces in guts and have it over. But one of us said, *Are there even grizzlies around here?* And we were again just useless men left to wishing we'd been born more impressive animals.

We shuffle in pairs through the front door. The buzz on our tongues from the language has stilled. Our mouths are those of a hungover. We push couches and chairs to the walls and sit in pairs on the floor. Every other time, one of us is the child. We wedge our bottoms into our father's lap. Our backs lean into fronts and we rest in its rise and fall. We've chosen our favorite books, so the father reads and we feel the vibration of their words in the cave of our chest. After stories, we connect the edges of a puzzle while father works out the mess of the middle. We complain when he says time to brush our teeth, ask him to please squeeze the paste, and help us floss those way back teeth. We swear we aren't tired when he pulls back the covers and lowers us. We are in the last seconds of wakefulness when he finishes the songs, so his kiss on our forehead is more dream than not.

When we dream, we dream ourselves fathers of living children. We drive them to their art class. We take them to the pool and launch them into belly flops. There is pizza, of course, and ice cream, but sometimes there is just eggs and toast and dropping off at school. Our dreams, impossibly, resist metaphor and symbolism. We wake with no inclination to try to explain them. They don't etch new neuropathways to make the real tolerable. They wedge into those too familiar to make a memory.

We wake to fog. We can't see the edge of the property, the station wagon, not even the last stair on the porch. The air mists in our lungs until it dissolves. We sit in the hammocks, wiggle until we are lost in the folds. Our stomachs quease with the hammock's gentle sway, and we wonder if we might have an accident. One of us is crying so all of us do.

Though we've imagined revenge, we just want to ask them some questions. We swear to ourselves, nothing more. Some days we fantasize they wake us with the moist heat of their lips on ours. They straddle us, and we are inside them without time to crave it. Their breasts sit high on their chests, firm and full of milk. They wait until we can't say no then ask for forgiveness. We are deep in the shame of the fantasy, our underwear warm and wet, when guilt sets in. We change our clothes without speaking. There is no one here to hold us accountable.

When the sun dissolves the fog, we see her sitting on the steps. She leans with bend of third trimester. We aren't sure which one she is—her face isn't toward us, but we know she is our own by the shape of her belly. Some imagine the dark red EKG of stretch marks, some marvel at the body's ability to stretch without trace. We see the bottom of navel risen, the lump of our infant's elbow or knee, the flinch of in utero hiccups.

How can this be? We've been so careful, one of us asks. The respite of recognition dissolves and we are again only our failures. We tell ourselves there's no way the baby is ours, we know better, we know what the mothers are capable of. We point at each other, faces full of *How could you?*

She stands, steps cautiously down the stairs. The hand railing leans and croaks with her weight, and we add it to the list of To-dos. *Careful!* We say, and rush the stairs. Some of us prepare the living room with pillows and footstools and towels rolled just right to support the lumbar. We make tea full of raspberry and nettle leaf. We fill a pouch with hot water to put wherever she feels cold. We scrape foods from plates we don't remember using. We pick up clothes we swear we didn't wear. We clear the hallway and use the shoe tree for shoes. We brush our teeth in case we have something to say close up. There is always the possibility this time will be different.

Welcome! We say. We wait for her to turn toward us. *We're ready for you!*

She stops at the bottom of the steps. Our mouths resist our swallow and our throats are full of pulse. We see our children as we last did. We look through their clothes for the favorite outfit, find the lovies they could never sleep without. We don't resist the thoughts of what we'd do to her to give our children another chance. It doesn't matter, of course. She's gone, there's nothing on the steps but an amniotic trail.

The sun has sharpened the edges of our property. We see mushrooms at the base of an alder. We see a split fencepost we never before noticed. We see the flattened grass the size of a resting deer. She is so gone we aren't sure she was there. We hear the quick *pap pap pap* of car's horn and circle the house to the barn. The station wagon is gone. One of us tears at his hair, blood streams from his scalp. We surround him. *You can't blame yourself,* we say. *You did everything you could,* we say. *We would stamp the pain out of your fucking skull if we thought it would help,* we think.

We watch him walk toward the road we can't see but must be there because we got here. His clothes are drenched, his shoes splug with each step. He slouches with the burden of a haunted.

Because he is us, he grows taller and shorter, husky then fat. His hair in a slop, then pricked into ice, clothes cricked with freeze. He vomits without aim. The seat of his pants droops. We hear what could be cry for mercy, or the opposite, and wait for something to end him. *Maybe he won't be back,* someone says, and we give them shut-the-fuck-up faces. We look away before he's out of sight.

Snow drops from the sky in heavy plops. We aren't dressed for winter, but we can't bring ourselves to go back inside. We pile twigs and branches and leaves, drag logs to sit on. We move closer to one another we say because of the cold. We feel the heat from the fire before we notice the steel wool and a flint in our fingers. We breathe in the first wisp of smoke. Branches lean and flames do to them what flames do. One of us brings the wheelbarrow, still full of hornets' nests. How could we have left so much unfinished? We hear the popping and clicking of the larvae, demanding to be fed. We dump them into the fire. Some hornets bolt from the nests, the scent of the dead strong on their tongues, and attack the bare of our arms and legs. Others burrow deeper, heat-toward. What we decide is the queen emerges, her flight like something underwater. She threatens our throats. We still until she lands on a log. We whack her, but our aim isn't what it once was, and our hearts aren't in it. We watch her drag her flattened thorax to the edge. We think of flicking her into the fire, to her young whose clicking and popping is now only a hiss, but this is not about revenge. We think of flicking ourselves in it, but this is not about relief. Nobody makes a move. Her whole body is a breath, and we watch her watch us. We have so much left to do to make things right.

The Reliever

I remember the first taking—it was much easier than I expected. I waited for an hour after the father left, then pressed the security code, predictably the child's birthday. Inside, the mother stood in the living room, the carpet at her feet a planet of wet dark. The baby, who'd been screaming, was now quiet. The mother faced the front window, which showed an expanse of grass that had been mowed into diminishing squares before becoming a single blade. When I took the baby, only the damp handprints of its mother still clung to the blanket.

I laid the baby in the crook of my arm, tapped his bottom lip with my fingertip, and his mouth received me. I realized then I'd been holding my breath, and my exhale eased the pressure at my temples. I felt the topography of his palate, each ridge as unique as its valley. There was a flash of calm in the baby's eyes before their blue became white and the lids dropped. This calm didn't last. My finger revealed its uselessness, and I noticed shit had slipped from the collar of his pajamas and the hair at the nape of his neck was slick with it.

We left the mother to her peace, hands poised as though they still held the weight of the baby. Her face was different— the canyons between her eyebrows had surfaced and her lips, once a strained into a horizon of pale, were maroon and moist. I followed her gaze once more; the bleached sky was defined only by the Evergreens that refused the demand of fall.

I lifted the inflatable blue bath into the main tub, spread a towel on the tile, and flattened any folds. I lay the baby on the towel and unzipped his pajamas. Tiny red rockets launched by the dozens over the stars and moon and planets of the fabric. A clip folded the baby's umbilical cord into a tiny blackened nub. When the yellow duck thermometer read OKAY, I lifted the baby into the bath. His legs bent and straightened in quick jabs before their stilling. I slid my fingers up and down the bony staircase of the spine, then cradled his head in my palm and gently washed away the waste.

After I'd set the hair dryer to low and dried the baby's various creases and folds, I fastened a diaper and zipped him into a new pair of pajamas. This pair, like the other, depicted an outer space scene: astronauts with moon-boots and dome-heads stood huge like the gods of tiny planets.

Downstairs his mother stood in the same spot, but I didn't pause to see which world she looked out on. I set the baby in its car seat, making sure the fit was loose enough for two fingers to fit between the strap and the bird flutter of its chest. She spoke then: *Atticus's diaper bag is in the hall closet,* and we were on our way.

Though I'd braced myself for the incessant fuss of the infant, Atticus slept soundly in the car. His snore was soft and inconsistent, and he grunted from the memory of having been born.

I don't know how long the mother stood there, lost in the relief of empty arms. Perhaps she was still standing there when her husband got home from work. Perhaps she saw him coming up the walkway, popped the cap from a beer and let him take a good, long drink before lifting her arms, warm with the memory of the baby, asking *Can you hold him so I can make dinner?* Perhaps they lived like that forever—the damp heat of the baby trapped in the crooks of their elbows, the mealy tang of breastmilk settled in their nostrils like a virus your body learns to tolerate.

I'm not naive. Alternate endings cross my mind as they would any other. The lack of her resistance undoes her. Perhaps she stamped her foot and tore in two. Perhaps she ate until her stomach burst. Or her windpipe collapsed from the force of the father. I didn't stay with these thoughts for long—I had a baby to take care of, after all.

I took Charly without really meaning to. Or rather, I hadn't planned it as carefully as I had with the first—mapping the times of the father's departures and returns, researching formula for the one most like a mother's milk, the tiny tool to clip and lift away nails the size of eyelashes. I wanted that baby, I won't deny that, but first there was an unwanting that allowed me to have him.

The night I took Charly I had driven a road that veined through hundreds of acres of corn. The baby, exhausted from a fit, was quiet as a breath. I was drawn to a driveway on the left, the way one is drawn to a wreck on the interstate. I drove along, stiffened my neck against the jerk of potholes. My knock on the screen door went unanswered, so I opened it and silenced the squawk with a slam.

Charly stood at the sink peeling the shell from a hard-boiled egg. Its scent flooded the room like a disaster. Vomit threatened my throat undeterred by my swallow. He looked at me, then to the stairs that moaned under the feet of his mother. He ate the egg whole, left the house, and I heard the car door click open and slam shut.

His mother was a shadow on the stairs before a body. I knew I should go—Charly was the only reason to be in the house, but then she was there, naked, one hand on her breast, the other lost in the dark between her legs. She stared at me as the movement of her hands became more frantic and forceful. I had every intention of leaving, I swear it, and maybe in another version I did. She approached me, and I collapsed under her. Fingers, slick with her, guided mine into her body. She pressed her nipple against my lips, told me to suck. The car alarm sounded, and its lights flashed, but I moved my fingers and tongue until her orgasm pulsed around my fingers, her eyes wide open, mouth closed against rush of breath.

The alarm's throbbing evened into a solid wave of sound. She lifted her body off mine, slipped into a dress made for a woman twice her size, and ascended the steps into the shadow. Her scent was all over me, but how it happened I have no idea.

In the car, I eased Charly's head from the belly of the horn. He was covered in vomit and drool foamed and bubbled in the corners of his mouth. I folded the baby's blanket into a pillow and wedged it between Charly's head and the window. I backed down the driveway until the house was no more than a smudge of light against the sky.

I took this position because I needed the work. But I must be clear—it was never my goal in life to be this kind of person. The stranger around the dark corner, at the grocery story, in the closet. The only person without a child at the playground. I don't actually like children. I didn't even want my own, let alone anyone else's. But people rarely choose who they become. Only a person with the right amount of damage can pull it off—and even still the shelf life of a Reliever is short. It's rare that I get to speak to the mothers, but when I do, the restraint it takes to resist sharing my story is great. It throbs at the back of my throat, pricks my skin with the want of the tell.

I kept the window down to air out the car. Charly, miraculously, was awake and watching the car force itself into the dark nothing in front of us. We'd have to talk about it, but not now. A rock dinged the windshield. A raccoon was dead on the roadside. Somewhere, daylight choked the dark from the sky and somebody was waiting for me to get back to work.

Sometimes months would pass between the takings. I'd watch the mothers exist as though I wouldn't need to visit them. They set up elaborate arts and crafts project for playdates. Arranged string cheese and pretzels into broomsticks for the class snack. Finally developed school photos and glued them into books to show that passage of time, as though just being alive was something to be proud of.

One of the mothers was a swimmer, so one day I followed her to the pool. She was a heavy woman, stretch marks squiggled the backs of her thighs and arms, suit worn thin on the seam. She always entered with a high dive, and I felt the sharp rungs of ladder deep in my soles as she climbed. Her dive shattered the water into a tantrum, but it settled quickly as she swam half its length under water. When she surfaced and started the crawl stroke, the water was barely rippled by her precise movement and the tiny sip of breath she took every fifth stroke. I sat unnoticed in the stands, my back rioting against the metal bleachers, my lungs heavy with the thick, moist air.

The mother lifted herself from the pool. The weight of her creaked the ladder. She was the type of woman people offered suggestions to about how to be a different type of woman. With some effort, she wiggled her feet into flip flops and retreated into the women's locker room. I didn't follow her there, of course, but I imagined her awkward undressing and her suit, twisting into an impossible equation, leaving its damp stamp on the locker room floor.

I was still in the bleachers when she emerged, brushed, seal-slick hair and in a black sweat suit. I followed her to her car, then with my car. I took a series of deep breaths to clear the sodden air from my lungs. She drove the speed limit or five under, flipped the blinker a hundred yards too early. I parked a block away from the school where I couldn't see but imagined Andrew's relief at her return—every drop-off the teachers pulling the child from her arms and her sung promise: *I'll always come back, I'll always come back I'll always come back to get you, I never could forget you.*

Once Andrew was strapped into his car seat, she handed him a snack: goldfish, halved grapes, cheese slices cut into heart shapes. I followed one car back on the road to the bay. We had to stop for a family of deer and I saw her point them out to her son. She crossed the railroad tracks and drove through the chain and onto the beach, where weeks earlier hundreds of jellyfish beached. Their bodies, transparent aside from the violent maroon nervous systems, constellated the shore. They only had eight hours on the beach before the sea reclaimed them, but crowds of people had visited them, children poked their bodies with sticks and sandaled feet while their parents warned them to stay back, *Even dead they can still sting you.*

I watched her emerge from the waves, her movement slowed only by the drag of the sweat suit. I waited until she'd climbed the stairs to the road, then released Andrew from the constraints of the car seat, his head lolling on my chest. His hair, the same slick black of his mother's, dripped the sea down the front of my shirt. He coughed up something black and slick, and I wiped his face clean with my sleeve. I strapped him into my car, covered him with towels and cranked the heat. The train announced its approach, so we waited behind the safety arm.

Andrew began convulsing; Charly reached into the backseat and held his hand and he stilled. The car was full of ocean, which meant nothing other than what it meant.

Before I took this job, I delivered the mail. My route was simple, three county blocks of addresses, Terrell Road to Mt. View to Elder to Barr. I used my own car, sat in the passenger seat and drove with my arm stretched across to grip the steering wheel. The neighborhood was the same as any other in that area. Kids hung upside down from branches of cherry trees, heads inches from the pavement. They bolted across the road without looking, pinched Black Cat firecrackers between their fingers seconds too long, pointed Roman candles at each other and lit the fuses. They drove drunk on New Year's, crashed, bodies rearranged in ditches the size of semis. They zipped from house to house, collecting habits and heartache and horrors. I knew them all, because I was one of them, and none suffered more than another until they did.

Andrew was only two days with me when I found Mary. I'd watched her mother before but had been drawn elsewhere. We saw her mother at the Shop & Go, cart full of nothing notable to someone other than me. Though I'd like to say she walked with the slouch of a woman capable of what she was capable of, she stood high, shoulders back and down like a yoga pose.

Mary rode in the cart, cheese whip coiled around her finger, lollipop bluing her teeth and lips. The groceries in the cart told me I had time until tomorrow. Though I'm usually a very healthy person, something revved low in my gut. I rushed to the bathroom, cutting it so close there was a brown streak on my underwear. The process was dramatic, like a practical joke, but when it was over, and I finally stood, blood pocked the toilet bowl. I folded toilet paper, wedged it in in case there was more blood. I searched the store for Mary and her mother, but they were gone.

I got into my car and drove east toward the mountains. I realized it had been years since I'd driven this highway. The area didn't have a name, it was just a stretch of road between two places, but I turned down a dirt road and parked the car in front of a trailer I hadn't seen from the road. An awning covered a picnic table and high chair, its tray scattered with peas, blueberries, and toast cut in squares. I picked up a sippy cup, sticky from a toddler's hands, and set it on the table. I knocked on the screen door and waited like a guest. The mountains were so bright against the blue of the sky I had to look away. I knocked again, then let myself in. The air was thick with the stench of bleach.

Mary watched me from the hallway, face as purple as a lollipop. When I held my hand to her, she grasped it with sticky fingers. I was expected to see her mother, so I opened the accordion door to the bathroom. Her mother was in the shower, and the room was full of steam and the scent of fake flowers. I flipped the fan switch and turned to leave. The shower door clunked open. Her mother's skin was streaked red from water far too hot. She hit me in the face with the bottle of shampoo, then kicked me in the crotch.

I'd been warned that some of them fight, but this was the first time I'd gotten any resistance. I wasn't allowed to fight back, so I lay on my back and surrendered. My testicles throbbed so I covered them, and she smacked my face with the hair dryer. Something unhitched inside my nose. A tooth dislodged too, and I felt its tinny socket with my tongue. There was a lull, so I opened my eyes. Her hand held a razor just inches from one of them. Though I tightened against it, a rush of blood spread over my underwear.

Mary was there when I was again aware, her fingers, still sticky, clasped in mine. Her breathing was wet and fractured with blood. Her face was gray aside from the blood around her mouth. I stood, steadied myself, and lifted her. I wiped blood from her lips and chin, then held the cloth to my nose. Her mother was nowhere, so I grabbed a stuffed lamb from her Pack 'n Play and left. I lifted her sippy cup, and the tablecloth beneath it had been bleached from the cup's dripped liquid.

Warmth spread onto my hip where I held Mary from blood that could've been mine but wasn't. I strapped her into the car. When she smiled at me, I saw the muscle of her tongue instead of skin. I buckled her into the car seat between Atticus and Andrew. She giggled when Andrew held the lamb up to his face and spoke to her in a voice quivered by bleats.

For the first time since I took this job, I sobbed. I was covered in shit, vomit, snot, and blood. I couldn't tell which mess was mine and which was that of the children. Most Relievers only lasted a year. I'd made it almost two but wasn't sure what that said about me. Did these children need me? Did their mothers?

We drove east past signs pleading, *Need a Rest? Take a Break, In Memory of Jonathan Reynolds, age 7* and *Drive Sober, Your Children's Lives Depend on It, Ashley & Ember Anderson.* It started to snow, and the elevation gain pressed into my ears like underwater. I stopped sobbing and paid attention to keeping my tires in the path already established. The road snaked around the side of the mountain, and the familiar quease of car sickness surged. I pinched the pressure point on the skin between my thumb and pointer finger as someone had once suggested, but my mouth filled with spit so I pulled over and vomited into the snow.

The fresh air steadied my head and I followed a set of footprints before I thought not to, and that is how I found Sarah and Nathan. A lack of oxygen had blued their lips and slivers of ice speckled their eyelashes. I lifted Sarah first, who was covered with Nathan's coat and pressed her face against the warmth of my neck. When I gently bent her legs at the hip, there was a sound like a dog's teeth against a bone.

Nathan's body, only covered with a long-sleeve T-shirt and jeans, resisted all movement when I lifted him. I put him in the front seat closest to the blast of the heater. Theirs was the first taking where I hadn't seen their mother. I knew better than to wonder if there had been some mistake in what drew me to them—their story was the same as any, and if they ever got a chance to tell it, how would they find the language to do so?

Outside, the world was more snow than sky. I drove with the caution of a school bus driver, turned Nathan's face toward the heater. His pale and waxy fingertips blued from the warmth, the horizon of his lips slackened, and I wiped the windows with my sleeve when the thaw of his body fogged them.

The Criteria

The stack is short today. I should be able to get through it before my lunch break and distribute a bit early. Though the criteria are always subject to change, they have been static for three months, so I no longer need to refer to the guidelines Dr. Powers left locked in the desk drawer on my first day. My office is windowless— it used to serve as an examination office at a gynecology clinic. Before I began working here, Dr. Powers replaced the exam table with a desk and chair, and the posters of the growth of a fetus, STDs sprouting like mushrooms, and black-and-white illustrations of reproductive anatomy with those with the current slogans about community, purity, and nutrition. I'd been in the office as a patient numerous times before, stared at each poster while Dr. Powers measured and scraped and estimated while the lights buzzed in a fractured *Om*. I'd always found the lack of natural light eerie, like people outside were healthy and living and hopeful and those inside vulnerable and waiting for the blood work to doom, or the ultra sound technician to let a "Huh," slip out, but now I find comfort in the fluorescence. This isn't the real world. Just an artificial in between. Temporary.

Before I count this week's applications, I guess that there are twenty-five. Upon counting, there are twenty-two. The first round of eliminations is based on age: families with parents twenty-five and younger are dismissed. Dr. Powers believes the young are less likely to understand the importance of exclusively organic nourishment. The next round is based on the number of minor dependents: any more than three results in dismissal (unless the family contains a single parent): people who've chosen to have more than three children exhibit a lack of awareness and respect for resources. The last round is based on health: those with any personal or family history of cancer, diabetes, gluten or diary allergies, heart disease or autoimmune deficiencies are dismissed. We haven't yet had to resort to physical tests, (Dr. Powers understands what can be revealed and intuited through blood pressure, heart rate, weight, eyesight, etc.) but Dr. Powers believes it may soon become necessary as the number of applicants increase. These questions are also the last ones listed on the application. Dr. Powers says people lie during times of need and having them answer these questions after they've answered a slew of less important ones encourages the truth. Sometimes the applicants wedge irrelevant information into the boxes to gain empathy (I cannot blame them, there is much need and much suffering) but I don't read their desperate scribblings. It simply isn't my job to compare and assess tragedies.

Up until this point, I haven't had to consider anything beyond the criteria I've mentioned, but after the first three rounds I must use a less objective selection process—Dr. Powers leaves it up to me. It wasn't like that in the early months—she used to have me submit the applications that weren't eliminated by the first three rounds. She'd said, "It will tear you up, let me be the one who gets destroyed," but it hadn't really been a problem. I haven't yet regained my ability to feel intensely about anything for more than a flash of a second now and again. I understand completely what is supposed to make me sad, angry, happy, discouraged, and so on, but I don't get the sting from the urge to cry, the acceleration of the heart from anger, or the need for the breath you have to take before a fit of laughter. There are moments when something reminds me of a time when I did feel, but they are so quick I barely feel anything before it dissipates. It is like holding a piece of grass to an electric fence—a zap of emotion before you tear your hand away with only a memory of the shock.

Today I only have to reject five applications. I used to read them carefully, hoping some sort of intuition would guide me and I would just know who most needed it. It never did. I'd made the same assumption when I was pregnant and hopeful for the intuition rumored to accompany motherhood. But after Atticus was born my intuition told me every cough was TB, each rash a symptom of meningitis, every fever a resurgence of the assumed eradicated polio. So now I am reckless with the applications. I make choices based on aesthetics—what kind of name is Cyril? Writing in all caps suggests a dominant and aggressive personality. A January birthdate? Winter's children are always so dark. If that fails, I just close my eyes, make a mess of the applications and choose. I do not look closely at the ones that are dismissed during this round. I simply stamp them as such.

I take my first break mid-morning. I've got two offerings scheduled and they will be waiting for me in the bathroom at ten. As usual, I find the adults swaying back and forth, shooshing fussy babies, wedging their faces deep into the infants' blankets or necks to avoid eye contact. There is such shame in not being able to care for your own. I empathize with them, but I cannot feel tenderness when I loosen the babies from their grip, or offer the soothing circular touch on their backs telling them I'm not here to judge. This month it is a woman too old for an infant, and an infant in a front pack on its father, head craning toward me and away from its father's useless chest. I've pulled a chair into the handicap stall and brought in a pillow that rests in a C around my middle. I can do both at once this way, letting nothing go to waste.

Though they are now calloused, there was a time when nursing felt like holding a flame to my nipples. The nurses at the hospital had told me it was all about the latch—get that right and nursing would feel as natural as breathing. They had cupped the back of my baby's head and directed his mouth onto my nipple. Squeeze it flat, they'd say, squishing my areole. Imagine it's a huge hamburger you're trying to shove into the baby's mouth. My baby devoured the colostrum, peeling off the top layer of my nipple within the first twenty-four hours. Once my milk came in the nurses offered pads to soak up the milk from the unused nipple, but I refused. While the prickly rush of let down surged into Atticus's mouth, the other breast's milk fountained before it slowed to drip and then nothing.

The woman and the father wait outside the stall as I had asked them too. I hear them washing their hands, the eek of the soap dispenser and hiss of the water amplified by the room's tile floor. When they finally settle down, I close my eyes and focus on the mouth on each nipple. Some days I almost remember a serenity I never had with my own.

After the infants have nursed themselves full, I pass them back to their people, though I want to feel the warmth of their spit up soak into my shirt and smell the tang of their breastfed shit. After one particularly long nursing session, I'd held Atticus up to my shoulder to burp him. Before I'd gotten his mouth positioned over my shoulder he'd spit up, his hot thick stream launched into my mouth. He looked at me as if, for the first time, he understood I was separate from his body. And though I wanted to have a mother-child moment of understanding his spit was mine, we were one, it was no different than swallowing my own saliva, I threw up into the burp cloth.

I am back to work in half an hour and onto processing, notification, and distribution. I meet Dr. Powers in her office to drop off the names of the chosen recipients and for my exam. Dr. Powers will prepare the documents that will be presented to the recipients after distributions. She believes they are more likely to agree after they've seen the nourishment they're being provided. The recipients must sign away certain rights and agree to certain terms before receiving the food. I know nothing of these arrangements, but trust they are necessary as Dr. Powers is a very intelligent and important woman and she understands matters of many sorts. She is one of the few doctors left in our region, and I am one of the few mothers. I am special, she tells me. I'm not sure about the specifics of her research, but she says what she does is crucial. After Dr. Powers helped deliver my two babies, one healthy and alive and the other neither, she stitched me up so well nurse after nurse commented on my incision while they dabbed salve over the wound. "Dr. Powers is the best at this," they said, peeling back the gauze. "You're lucky to have her."

Some days she simply takes my pulse and blood pressure. Other days I'm asked to disrobe and get onto the exam table and cover up with the paper sheet. She moves quickly, and she apologizes for the coldness of her hands and instruments. I often see other women from the Accepteds list come and go from her office. Like I said, there are certain obligations that come with being chosen.

"The stack is short this week," I say. Today is an "internal" day, so I take a deep breath, exhale to let the speculum enter. "Sometimes I think that means something."

"It will," she says. I hear the light of her instrument click on. "How are your offerings?"

"Fine." Today's baby on the left had opened its hand and pressed its palm against my breast. I had closed my eyes to chase the flash of Atticus and for a split second the flutter of its fingers was his.

"Can you tighten around my fingers?"

I squeeze into a Kegel.

"Good. Everything still looks great. Healthy."

Dr. Powers peels back the sheet and cups my right breast with both hands, moving in shrinking circles until her gloved fingers lightly pinches my nipple. She repeats the process on the left. I feel the prickly rush of milk and think of my two-o-clock recipients, who will soon enter the bathroom and wait for me.

"How many are you doing these days?"

"Four a day," I lie. I'd recently added two: 7 a.m. and 7p.m.

"You know it's unlikely they will survive without other nourishment. I know you know that." When she's finished checking my breasts, she attaches the Velcro of the gown to cover me. When she looks at my face, I nod and imagine the sting of tears I should feel.

"You look thin. Your neck and cheeks. Start taking an extra box for yourself. It's crucial you stay well."

The two-o-clock feedings take longer than usual. I've nursed the one on my left breast for the past three weeks, but today each time I turn her mouth toward my nipple she twists her face away. The baby on my right sucks with quick consistency, not at all disturbed by the fussing of the other. When I let down and the milk sprays, I press her face close and close her lips around my nipple. This is not a time for waste.

I'd held my dead baby in the crook of my right arm for an hour while I nursed the living one. I expected to love both of them immediately, as I'd been told every mother did, and that I would find them beautiful no matter what. And Atticus was perfect, but the other one felt heavy and moist in my arm and I just wanted him gone. He'd almost killed Atticus, gorging himself on nutrients while his twin slowly starved. I passed him to my husband and tickled Atticus' cheek with my finger like they had shown me to keep him awake while feeding. Though Dr. Powers had concerns about Atticus' ability to nurse considering his small size, he latched on quickly and nursed like the starving baby he was.

The sickness had come on gradually, usually taking a month or so to kill. I noticed people dying around me, of course, or heard of it, but I had problems of my own. Atticus wouldn't sleep for more than an hour and a half at a time, and sometimes I'd go three or four days with no more than a thirty minute nap. My husband helped as best he could, but Atticus was just too hungry. When the neighbors, a couple in their seventies, died within hours of each other, I watched their emaciated bodies bob by on a single stretcher. I understood it was a shame, but I felt nothing. I baked a casserole as people do, but there was no one to give it to.

After the two o'clock offerings I take the stack of the Accepteds to the waiting room and make the announcements. The room's décor, like that of my office, has been altered, though the wallpaper still reads *It's A Girl!, It's A Boy!,* surrounded by tiny footprints, baby bottles, and pacifiers. I'd found it distasteful even before the illness, and recently gotten permission from Dr. Powers to paint over the wallpaper.

The applicants are rarely seated. They lean, backs or shoulders against the walls, some bent with their arms resting on the reception desk. I read the names loudly then spell each name slowly to avoid false hope and confusion. I'd once read "Mortensen" and had to turn the "Morgensen" family away at after they'd waited in the receiving line, laughing with caution and relief and chatting with the others about finally getting some good luck. It is from the *Dismissed* that I choose the recipients of my offerings. Now that I've added two offerings a day, I can feed four more babies a day, a total of eight in a twenty-four-hour period. They of course need supplemental nourishment, but the antibodies and immunities my breast milk gives them is invaluable. Or at least better than nothing. I do what I can.

I lead the Accepteds to the distribution garage. As usual, they are giddy—a visible lightness in their movement, airy talk about the weather, but they are also jumpy, jerking if a door slams, gasping if I quickly turn and speak. Dr. Powers has a family of three adult sons, two of whom have survived, and they join me in the garage in case things ever become dangerous. I call each family's name in alphabetical order, and they climb into the truck and lift their box. Each family member thanks me again and again and though I understand their gratitude, that they need to feel like I understand how degrading it is to beg for food for one's family, I can only nod. I don't deserve gratitude.

After the distribution I return to my office and collect my things and meet Dr. Powers in her office. On days of internal exams, she insists on driving me home. Sometimes she reaches over and puts her hand over mine or on my leg. We don't talk much, but sometimes she'll sing and I'll hum along, though the way the vibration calms my heart aches my stomach.

I have two hours at home before my six o'clock recipients, so I peel a cucumber and heat some beans before I sit and look at the calendar. It has been twelve days since I've seen my husband. It will be two more, assuming all is well. On his visit we made love twice between my ten and two offerings. He was so gentle I could barely feel the weight of his stomach and chest touching mine, or the coolness of the air drying the sweat from our bodies. We lay in bed, his hand cradling my breast as it filled.

It wasn't until he said I had to tell him if I ever felt like hurting Atticus that I'd realized what I'd imagined doing wasn't normal. I'd heard of women who'd killed their children, holding child after child under the bathwater until they stilled, buckling them into carseats and sending the car off the end of a pier. These were tangible horrors, all too possible. I'd imagined stuffing Atticus into a bottle like a ship, seeing his face smashed ugly by the glass, dipping his body into wet cement to keeps his bones from being broken. I thought it too strange not be normal.

The last day Atticus and I had stood at the window watching my husband walk the sidewalk toward the car. I was thinking about the weeds burrowing through the cracks in the cement when I noticed one of his pantlegs tucked into the back of his sock. Atticus was nursing, and when I knocked on the window and bent down to pull at my pantleg, he'd ripped his mouth away from my nipple and his head fell back. I saw the shiny inflammation in his neck crease, crumbles of spit up trapped within layers of fat. I brought his neck to my face and breathed in. The scent was rancid, how I imagined his decaying body would smell. I took another deep breath, etching it into memory. I looked back out the window and saw my husband kneeling to fix his pantleg and thought I should give Atticus a bath.

When he returned hours later, his pantleg was fine, but his zipper was down, which made me smile. He watched me on his walk up to the house, I mouthed your zipper and pointed, but his mouth was a line and I realized suddenly how cold I was. When he got inside, he took Atticus and I saw that the back of his pajamas was soaked to the neckline in shit. Andrew pointed to the floor and said something I didn't hear. I turned away and stepped into what must've been the mess from my own body. I hadn't moved for the eight hours he had been gone. Or if I had, I had no memory of doing so.

I peel a second cucumber and eat it. I should try some of the cheese, protein is crucial for me to continue my offerings, but some days I can't shake the worry. So much depends on my milk, and though there hasn't been a case reported from any of the recipients, the risk swells in my stomach like rotten meat. Tomorrow I will try it, I promise myself, but tonight it is cucumbers and black beans. I finish my meal, turn off the lights and heat and pull the car out of the garage. I give the seven o'clock offerings in my car in the parking lot of the hospital where there are always people in case something goes wrong.

These babies are the same as the others. They are, above all else, hungry. I have to sit in the back seat so there is room for each baby to comfortably feed. One of them is here with his mother who is well into her forties and will only speak to me through her infant, "Tobias is so grateful. Tobias really appreciates your offering. Tobias will never forget what you've done for him."

The mother hasn't been infected by the sickness, but the risk is too high, she was a carnivore, and not exclusive. She's a Dismissed.

The mother stares out the front windshield. I can see her reflection and notice she never looks at my face. My husband used to love to watch me nurse Atticus. If Atticus had slept well and was in a happy mood, I'd pull him off my nipple and let milk spray in his direction for a second. He would joke about how wrong it was to feel so turned on and we would be happy for a minute, me thrilled at his amazement of my body and him zapped by me feeling the thrill. There were other moments when Atticus would sleep in my arms and he would hold me and I'd feel content for just long enough to know that was how I should feel. Then it was gone.

After the last offering of the day, I drive home and run a bath. My breasts, deflated, bob on the water. I see my reflection and think of Tobias' mother staring out the window into nothing. I put my face underwater and resist the urge to breathe. I wash and groom my body so my husband will find it desirable. It is the least I can do. In bed I touch my body and imagine my hands are his—roughen my smooth palms into calloused, thin fingers into thick. I wait to feel something, even the slightest pulse, the slightest slip of wetness. But as usual there is nothing. I switch on the baby's video monitor and increase the volume so Atticus' empty room hums me to sleep.

The days after Distribution days are quiet. I sit at the receiving desk and hand out the occasional application. I've heard various theories about the best time to turn in an application. Some say submitting the day after Distribution shows an over eagerness, like things might be getting really bad so why bother nourish those past nourishment. Others claim it's best to wait until the day before Distribution so that yours will be on the top of the stack and reviewed first, before the tedium of the task has set in. Some believe none of that matters, and that the decisions are completely random.

I clean on these days: wipe down counters, pens, clipboards, chairs, windows and bathrooms with bleach. Early on, before we'd developed the proper exit procedures for the Dismissed there were a few instances of vandalism in the bathrooms. I felt nothing while I scrubbed and scraped the dirty slurs, curses, and damnations from the bathroom walls, but I imagined that I should probably feel shame.

Dr. Powers has approved my request to paint over the waiting room wallpaper, so after the cleaning I set to covering the furniture with the crinkly white paper sheets from the exam room and collecting the painting supplies. Dr. Powers has brought in some paint and brushes. The paint is a light sky blue, Calming and hopeful, she told me, Like a sunny day.

I paint until the next offering. The baby girl is again disinterested in feeding, though she doesn't fuss or twist away. Her tearless eyes stare at me, her lips fused against my nipple. I know this will be my last day with this one. When I let down, I don't force her to drink. My milk sprays her face with tiny white bullets. She will likely die by the end of the week. Though her mother and father will be seared with the pain of losing her, hate themselves, then me, then settle on hating each other, she will die never feeling sadness or loss or suffering or guilt.

After the offerings I return to painting. I decide that along with the beans and cucumbers I will slice some cheese and grill some beef for my husband's visit. It feels like it has been months since I've seen him and that it is a special occasion deserving of a real meal full of protein. On his last visit I spoke to him about my work with Dr. Powers, and how my offerings have kept up my production so that when Atticus returns he will have more than he could ever need.

Though my husband never mentions Atticus, he said he was proud of me for my progress and I think he may surprise me soon with a visit from him. It may take a bit, but I know he will again pick up nursing easily. As I close my eyes against the clinic's wallpaper, I imagine holding his body to mine, his head positioned perfectly at my breast to avoid a strain on his neck. His eyes will find mine, and perhaps his hand may even reach up toward my face. His mouth will open and lips enclose my nipple, and then, in that second before the prickly rush of milk surges I will again feel something so intense and beautiful and terrifying, as my milk explodes into his tiny mouth.

What the Earth Offers

The children sit at the kitchen table. Their eyes, fat with hope, glide from me to their plates to one another like they're underwater. The youngest, Mary, licks her finger, presses crumb after crumb onto the tip. She counts, she always counts, so I know when crumbs become crumb becomes stark white ceramic. The older, Micah, carefully blows a few of his crumbs onto her plate and she counts again.

They are good children. They will not ask for more than I have given them, one slice of buttered toast each, and they do not leave the table until I have eaten. I take my time. Relief saturates me as the arms of the chair wedge into the fat on my hips: tomorrow I will drag over the piano bench, on which my father and I once sat and sang songs while his fingers stumbled through our favorites: One Tin Soldier, Blow the Man Down, Clementine.

The children inhale deeply when I set my meal on the table: bacon, over-easy eggs, potatoes melting grated cheese, toast, their tongues desperate to translate scent into taste. There are people, I tell them, who have trained their bodies to survive on nothing but air. I can't remember if this is something I once read or if I made it up. The children each take a turn hovered over my plate. They inhale through their mouths, pause while the air sticks to their tongues, exhale and wait for relief from the gut clench of hunger.

After breakfast, they carry their plates to the counter and sit on the couch until I'm ready to read to them. They've noticed my body's slow growth, and the distance between them is farther than it has ever been. The center cushion slumps between them like an insult. There was a time when I would fuss about, wash dishes, sweep the floor, haul the compost to the pile outside before giving them my attention. Now I put their dishes in the sink and lower myself into the space. They've each chosen three books for me to read, and even though Micah can read on his own, I read each story, pausing so they can both study the illustrations, welcoming they "whys" and "how comes" about the characters' motivations, settings where the characters draw their own surroundings, the endings where wrongs are righted.

Today the earth is still, but over the past few weeks I've heard the rumbling in the earth's gut— its threat clenched my stomach like food poisoning. Some days framed pictures shiver on the wall and glasses clank in the cupboards. We've been warned for years about the inevitability of the earth rupturing and described to in detail the destruction and despair that would follow. We are each day closer to this than the one before. The children don't seem to notice. They listen to the stories without distraction, the bones of their legs parallel the fat of mine. I keep my voice stable, read the words without listening, imagine scenarios of children sucked out to sea or swallowed by the split-open earth.

After the books we go outside so I can work on the shelter while they play in the yard. I've set up a nature scavenger hunt. They must collect pine cones, pillbugs, sap, earthworms, slugs and dandelions. I've drawn pictures of each on construction paper and included facts. Slugs and snails must be stored in a plastic bag for twenty-four hours before eaten. Pill bugs are crustaceans and must be boiled first. Sap can seal a cut and prevent infection. Earthworms are higher in protein than chicken or beef.

My father taught me much of this survival information when we went camping and on our long walks through our twenty-five-acre property. We'd spend hours scouring the forest's floor for the telltale tenting of leaves at the base of alder trees. I was terrible at gathering the mushrooms, constantly stamping them flat or kicking off their heads to my father's low *Goddammit*. I'd seen him eat earthworms, pillbugs, grubs, and ants he claimed tasted like lemons. At first I thought he was tricking me and I'd squeal with delighted disgust, but he ate them long after I'd stopped giving any sort of reaction.

Micah skirts the edge of the lawn and holds the hem of his T-shirt to carry the items he collects. Mary trails behind him, picking up the things he drops carefully enough for her to think she's found them. His kindness frightens and confuses me, and I want to tell him to keep what he finds for himself and let her find on her own what the earth offers. She lifts a white grub from the grass, rests it in her palm. She sniffs it, tosses it onto the ground, and points to the mess it has made in her palm. Each item on the hunt has nutritional or survival value she will learn about from the flashcards I've made, but for now it is only another living being she doesn't understand.

The shelter was built in 1983, and we were waiting to become permanent shadows on sidewalks, street corners, or the concrete walls of whatever buildings we were walking past when the push of a button stamped us irrelevant. Though my father swore we would in no way want to survive a most likely Soviet attack, that summer we spent Saturday mornings at the local library: me, desperate for the next book in the series about the joys and heartbreaks of perfect blond twins living in a sweet valley, him researching the techniques, strategies, and testimonials about how to stay alive after a disaster.

I open the shelter's door to the sour, earth scent of home-canned carrots, beets, tomatoes and green beans that once lined the shelves of the shelter, keeping us free from the poisons of store bought vegetables until late spring. I never admitted it to my father, but I'd longed for the colorful labels glued to aluminum cans at the grocery store, the curvy font of the mass produced instead of my father's all caps Sharpied scrawl, as if we couldn't see the contents through the glass jars.

I now know this shelter would've done little to protect us from a nuclear attack. We would've been exposed to radiation, and slowly, or not so slowly, suffered diarrhea, vomiting, pulled our hair out in brittle chucks, died a worse death than being killed by the initial explosion. But today's fears are different. Earthquake, tsunami, plague. Some will survive. They will suffer greatly, likely at the hands of one another, but they will survive.

The shelter will provide a place where the children might thrive, even if stuck in hiding for an extended amount of time. I read the only toys a child needs to be brilliant are blocks, balls, and books, so of course there are those, but I've also piled their cots with things they've loved: a stuffed giant squid, a toy kangaroo with a baby in its pouch, a set of magnetic blocks, vitamins disguised as multi-colored candy bears. I'm working now on ambiance—children deserve some happiness in the depths of suffering. I painted it a calm shade of green, and animal trinkets line the shelves where the jars once sat. Horses drink from tiny troughs while others gallop through forests of tiny plastic trees. Zebras, elephants, and tigers line the wall on the other side of the shelter, the most violent animals slink behind fences.

Last week I dragged out the old worm box to make room for Micah's cot. I'd felt the earth rumbling too many times that day and the threat of the time nearing wedged in my throat like a bone. Again, the children didn't seem to notice, but I've always been more sensitive to even the slightest movement of earth. Each spring, my father and I would creep onto the lawn after the ground had been soaked by rain or the green sprinkler he'd set on a sawhorse. He'd lightly press his body to the ground, my own a miniature version of his. If you're quiet enough, he'd told me the first time, you can hear them rising. And he was right. Their tiny pink heads emerged, and once there was enough visible, he'd carefully pinch it and coax the body free. My first time, worm after worm recoiled from my touch. I pinched some in two. Eventually I learned the perfect strength I needed to exert to pull, and then the worms offered themselves.

After I've arranged the wolves and grizzlies around the laminated lake stocked with goldfish crackers, my watch tells me it's time for my mid-morning meal. I'm never hungry, so I rely on it to remind me when ninety minutes have passed. Outside, blooming lilacs have sweetened the air and I pause for a moment and let it flush out the must of the shelter. I make a hand-to-mouth motion to Micah and Mary, who are inch high on the edge of the woods.

After they wash their hands, they wait. Hope fattens their pupils. Though they've been on the edge of starvation for weeks, they are resilient—the lack of nourishment has trained their bodies how to survive on very little. I prepare their snack: two celery sticks, half a carrot stick and a grape arranged into a strange face on their plates. Each has a teaspoon of peanut butter that completes the mouths. They lean over the plate, noses hovered above the peanut butter, and inhale. They eat the celery first, which I've told them uses more calories to digest than it provides, so it consumes their bellies' fat and not the food they put in it.

For myself, I've saved the bacon fat from breakfast to melt over two baked potatoes. The butter and fat warm the sour cream. I place my plate under each of their noses and again they inhale. When I return the plate to my placemat, the butter has spilled over the edge of the potato. It runs in a pale yellow river toward the side of the plate. The water in my glass quivers. I close my eyes and listen for the hum of the earth's vibration. It is good the shelter is almost complete.

My father and I spent four days in our basement after the eruption of Mt. St. Helens. We were hundreds of miles away, but I swear we felt its blast in our teeth. Everyone had known it was coming, but most hadn't counted on strong currents winding its chalky ash up the corridor where it settled on cars, houses, and deep in the lungs of anyone who had to breathe. The basement did little to protect us. My father's cough raged soon after, and never calmed.

The children finish their meals quickly, but stay at the table. They watch the lift and lower of my fork, and their eyes plummet when a bite slips from my fork onto the table. My meal hovers at the back of my throat, but I swallow down another bite. When there are only the brown husks of the potatoes left, I push the plate away and wave them to me. I lift Mary onto my knee, and my fingers slip under her bottom ribs. Micah sits on the other leg, and his coccyx presses into the meat of my thigh. They've always been thin children. I've taken pride that—they aren't inclined to excess or waste—even as babies they'd nurse for only a moment or so after the milk surged into their mouths, never long enough to taste the fat-choked hind milk.

After our snack, I set them up for their hour of screen time. Today is Micah's day to choose from the shows I've brought him from the library, but he only chooses what Mary likes. They sit on their knees and watch two brothers search the world for the most unique and intriguing animals. They often share the things they've learned during their baths: Mama, did you know crocodiles carry their babies in their mouths? Some baby spiders kill their siblings and eat their mother? Isn't it amazing how things survive, I reply.

While the children are occupied, I retreat to my room and turn on the television. It's the show where the guests share a tragic experience, and the host offers insight about the path to healing. Today's show features a woman who drove her car into a lake. She describes the screams of her three children as harmonious. She tells the host she'd been drowning since the birth of her first, and when the children quieted, the pressure in her lungs released and she surfaced. She holds her hand in front of her mouth as she speaks, and the host repeats her words. He takes her hands in his, and her sob splits open her mouth, her teeth flare against the black hole of her mouth like ghosts. Though I mistrust the validity of many of these stories, I can't help but envy this woman. Her disaster is tangible. She knows what will undo her. She doesn't wait around and wonder when, how, why.

When it is time for lunch, I sit at the table and let the children prepare the food. Lunch is the biggest meal of the day for our family. Mary twists a cloth under steaming water and wipes the table off in slow horizontal swipes. Micah sets water to boil, pours Alfredo sauce into a pot. Ground sausage spatters fat onto the stovetop, which Mary will wipe clean after our meal. While my food cooks, Micah cracks two hard boiled eggs, one for him and one for his sister. He pinches and lifts each shell fragment carefully as not to lose any of the white. He rinses each egg, halves then quarters it, sprinkles salt until the yellow is paled by its translucence. Though his body obviously needs more sustenance than hers, he stabs a quarter of his egg and lets it fall from his fork onto her plate. This will kill him, I fear, this selflessness in opposition to survival, but I keep silent. You can't force a person to survive.

I set out puzzles for the afternoon activity, many of which I used to do with my father. They feature scenes of the wild: a salmon thrashes in the mouth of a grizzly; a five-point buck glares at the viewer while birds glide above in a perfect V. My father believed in the power of a puzzle, said there was only one right way to understand the scene before you. He often paused in whatever task he was engaged in, and scanned the scenery, his head turning in the slowest no. He'd ask me to tell him what I saw, and my heart thumped with the chance to get it right. The first time he asked, I answered *books* and *people*. He smiled, just the corners of his lips raised as if they were attached to hooks, and said, *Survive.* He pointed out emergency exits, first aid kits, listed items such as keyboards, extension cords, pencils— weapons are everywhere if you're willing to fight.

One puzzle features a typical mountain scene: granite peaks spear the blue smear of sky; pine trees are scattered in the meadow, scarlet lilies rage in their shade. The puzzle came from the gift shop at Diablo Lake—the image on its box long faded by the time we bought it—where we camped every summer. My father wove through the campground at five miles per hour until we found the picnic table with the flattest surface and after a long day on the lake, my skin ready to split from the sun, we'd hover over these puzzles, amped on Shasta. We'd work long into the night, squinting at the pieces in the flicker of the fire until our fingers were too numb from the cold to make the pieces fit.

Occasionally I'd jump at a sound in the night, bears and cougars common to the area, and my father would pat the gun on his side and tell me not to worry. Didn't I know he'd always keep me safe?

I believed him, and never complained about the many rules of safe-keeping. After a day of fishing, we'd sit on the end of the dock, slit open the pale bellies of fish and scrape the guts into the water. The water was shallow enough to watch the organs sink and separate before resting soundlessly on the bottom next to the pale and bloated bits of other fish. We grilled our day's catch at the group picnic spots far from our own campsite. We never brought any back to our camp—any more than we could eat was given away to others we'd seen on the lake, shaking fists or heads as we reeled them in—and we scrubbed our hands and faces with lake water and the soap in the foot of a pair of nylons my father kept in the boat.

The last time we camped together, I finally saw a grizzly. One morning I woke to my father's coughing fit. He pressed a pillow over his face, but I knew by the time it calmed I'd be too far from sleep to bother with it. I looked out the loft window of our camper. The sun had stained the sky behind the mountains pink. There was a split second understanding of this place as being the most beautiful in the world before movement at the campsite across from ours caught my eye, and I saw a grizzly, snout buried in the belly of what looked like a dog. I called my father, who climbed into the canopy to look out the window. It was clear whatever it was was long dead—the body lax, only moving in small jerks as the bear's muzzle submerged and surfaced from its guts.

I anticipated his question, *What do you see?* I watched the scene, waiting to feel a clench in my stomach or tears stinging my eyes. Nothing. I released my focus and looked around the campsite. A white garbage bag hung shredded and empty from the hitch ball of their truck. Two fishing poles leaned against the motorhome. A Styrofoam ice chest missing its lid. A frying pan sat on a camp stove. There was much more to assess, but I heard my father's scream: deep and low, from the gut, before it exploded into a shriek. His shotgun blasted, and the grizzly ran off. We'd never owned a dog, my father hated their smell, but he picked it up and he pressed his face into its neck. His screams were muffled. Its legs jerked with the movement of his sobs. That's when I saw it was wearing clothes. There was even a shoe dangling from its foot, the same kind I had at home, blue and white with a zipper on the side to carry coins. What the grizzly hadn't gotten to lay scattered around the site, and my father yelled at me to help him. I never finished with my survival assessment, and my father never again asked me to give one.

The children enter the kitchen and choose a puzzle. Micah slowly flips each piece picture side up as if they will reveal a secret. He works with the edges: corners first, then earth and sky. He tells his sister to do the same when she finds a deer's muzzle and searches only for its face. The room is so quiet, only the hesitant tap of a piece finding its place. I steep chamomile tea for them, pour it into the tiny tea set Mary found in the attic. I drink coffee, its black browned by the heavy cream, and watch them without critique or offering to help. My tongue wears the cream long after I swallow, and I doze.

I wake from a dream about waking up, getting dressed, and eating breakfast. I've never been cursed with the disorienting symbolism of dreams. I've held the children when they awoke, shivering from the horror of a near-death dream, rubbed their backs and rocked them until they again gave into sleep. I remember the shadows under my father's eyes, the lethargy of a body awake when it hasn't slept. I can't remember ever having had a dream that didn't simply depict every day activities.

The children have finished their puzzles. They flash by the window like things you think you saw but can't be sure. Though they are quite undernourished, they are still driven to play, still approach the world like it has something to do with them. They seem to experience hunger like they would a hangnail or a paper cut. Inconvenient, annoying, but nothing to make you stop living. I'm not even sure the locks I've put on the cupboards and refrigerator are necessary. They've finally learned to live on very little.

I wave to the children from the window and head to the shelter. I open the door and inhale the musty air. Behind the back wall, there is a smaller room once only accessed by unlocking three deadbolts. My father told me to stay out of it, but showed me where the keys were, just in case. I'd frequent the space in the summers, where the cool dark turned sweat into shiver. Here, he kept containers of water, guns and ammunition, five-pound bags of rice and salt, cases of Campbell's chicken noodle and tomato soup, and double zip locked Oberto beef jerky. In our house, we ate the store brand of these soups, and homemade salmon jerky my father hang-dried in strips. There were five-gallon buckets claiming to hold as many "meals" as to keep an adult alive for 365 days.

This back room's empty now, its door held closed only by a set of hook-and-eye latches I screwed into wood. The paint where the deadbolts clung has long flaked away, revealing the wood's natural hue, and the groove from the crowbar's arm has worn smooth. The doorway is so small I have to get on my knees to enter. The frame answers the expanse of my body with a *shhh*. The wall to the east, which would've welcomed an unobstructed view of the sun rising over Mt. Baker if it had boasted a window, is pocked with the misshapen *O* from the bullet's entry. I never saw the mess my father's death left, but my memory of it is sharper than any other. I see the flesh of his face sunken into his skull, the horrific grin of decomposition. I know things once solid liquefied, and the scent of him when he pulled me into a hug, or slung me one-armed onto his shoulders, the scent that told me we belonged only to each other, became putrid, toxic.

My watch tells me it's again time to eat. Getting through the door seems harder on the way out, and for a second I think I might not be able to do it. I feel the pinch of sweat under my arms, the hint of my throat collapsing. I take a slow, deep breath, the kind I imagined one would take if trapped underground with limited oxygen. The frame scrapes my sides, cricks with the effort, and releases me. Outside the shelter, Micah is spinning himself senseless and stumbling toward Mary, whose shrieks and squeals in laughter. Disequilibrium prevails, and he falls. He lies on his back, watches the sky spin in a fit above him. Mary splays her body like a star next to him. Though their hunger must be terrible, they don't move when I tell them it is time for their afternoon snack. They are still, backs flat against the earth, faces open to the sky.

The Concrete Underneath

Later, everyone would assume the shooter had missed their target. The bullet slid through Edna's throat and scattered chunks of skin, esophagus, and her inactive thyroid gland onto the refrigerator. Charles' first thought was of the damage to the appliance; they'd gotten a new model only two years back that had a water and ice dispenser and they were still paying it off. The shot surprised him—he'd squeezed his can of Schmidt so hard the bass being ripped from the river crumpled and he knocked two other cans (one featuring a five point buck, another a thrashing trout in a grizzly's maw) onto the floor. Their clank set his ears ringing. It was the gun shot, obviously, that had done that to his ears, but people often mistake the cause of one thing for that of another. Edna made a sound he would later describe as "guttural," and he realized she was alive. He moved toward her, but didn't touch her. She was still there; her pupils pricks of black in the blue, and he took a hand towel from the oven's handle and lay it across her throat.

"Jesus Christ, Edna. There's blood everywhere." Her head was angled toward the refrigerator, where photos of their grand-daughters were arranged chronologically. Teena and Tisha had horizontal records of their growth since kindergarten. Edna had just added the most recent photos earlier that afternoon. Charles had mentioned Teena looked like she was twenty, then held Tisha between his thumb and pointer finger until Edna had said "Leave her alone," and magneted it onto the refrigerator.

Teena would be entering high school in the fall, Tisha the sixth grade. Edna had noticed a mole just to the left of Teena's nose and wondered if it was real. Tisha's shirt collar was slightly folded inward on the right side. The pictures would of course now have to be disposed of.

Charles heard the screen door click shut, and wondered how the police had gotten there so quickly. Nobody entered; it was the county, gunshots were not unusual, especially in the summer when there were so many hours of daylight to fill. Everyone on their block owned guns. Some for hunting, some for fun, some for protection.

Charles called his daughter, Teresa.

"I think your mother's dead."

Mary Trapp, the neighbor to the east, felt the boom of the shot in her fillings. She had spent the past forty-five minutes looking for Christina, her twelve-year-old daughter with Down's Syndrome. Under normal circumstances her mother wouldn't have worried. There were woods and trails on their five acres, and she often hiked through them alone or with other neighborhood children. But a week earlier, Mary had interrupted Christina exploring her body in a way she hadn't expected, even though Christina's doctor had warned she was on the verge of womanhood. Mary remembered the power of this type of exploration—how it wandered even the most responsible and cautious girls into situations she worried Christina would not understand or be able to prevent.

The neighbors often discussed Christina, expressing surprise at her capabilities, her "almost normal" looks, and more recently her developing body seen as a disaster waiting to happen. They'd shake their heads, silently praising themselves for creating children with forty-six chromosomes. Charles had noticed Christina's development and knew she occasionally spent afternoons in his barn. She had long, thick blond hair that her mother spun into ringlets or whipped into braids. He couldn't stand its thickness, and when she shook it to free hay or a leaf, she looked like the woman on the Nice and Easy box his wife bought every three- to- four months to hide the gray. Christina was not on her family's property at the time of the shooting. She had climbed into Grandpa Chuck's hayloft. Neighborhood cats often meandered between the bails and collected the loosened hay into soft bundles to birth their kittens. The feline mothers seemed to understand Charles allowed his barn to become a manger for these strays—other neighbors weren't as accommodating, such as Jon Williams, who each spring filled a bucket with water and held kitten after kitten under until they stilled.

As with most children, Christina loved discovering a batch of fresh lives, writhing blindly until their mother's nipples silenced their mewing. Christina wedged her body between two bails, listening so intently for the tiny meows that when the bullet exploded she wet her pants, something she hadn't done in years. The air of the barn was so thick and warm she barely felt the urine blackening her blue jeans.

Jon Williams did not at all enjoy drowning kittens. When possible he'd lock the mother cat in the dog's pen, well out of view of the bucket, dump the dog's food into the grass and refill the bowl with the canned soft cat food usually saved for mashing de-wormer into. He felt the tiny scrawl of kitten claw against the plastic edge of the bucket in the deep unnamed part between his ear and throat. They were of course too weak to wiggle free from his grip, but he was careful not to squeeze their middles too hard during the last squirming of life.

Though his wife was always sure to have their daughters, Michelle and Joanne, away on these days, he knew them being able to choose one kitten from each batch to keep would soon not be enough for them to tolerate this getting rid of. Michelle, who was thirteen, had actually asked her mother if she could stay home for the most recent drowning. Though she'd always had a much higher tolerance for that which his wife and youngest daughter found gruesome, (at eight years old she slit open her just-caught fish, tugging out the organs and slapping them into the gut bin) he was firm she leave with her mother and not witness the drowning.

Jon heard the gunshot while dragging a homemade, three-pronged row-maker across his garden. He split-second paused—he had many guns, most of which he kept in a safe, but his revolver was in his nightstand. What good would a gun do if someone broke in and all his guns were locked up in a safe? The girls knew it was there, too, and he'd shown them how to use it last year when Dwayne Jeffries moved back into his parent's house across the street. Dwayne had been gone for five years, and though no one knew where for sure, Jon thought you could never be too careful. Dwayne's people weren't quite right, he thought, and though he believed people should mind their own damn business he carefully watched for any activity at the Jeffries house: a different car on the lawn, the flag on the mailbox up only moments before the mailman drove by, the thick scent of cedar smoke twirling from the chimney in non-winter months. The shot was a quarter mile or so away, John guessed, the girls were fine. He returned to thinking about which rows of the garden would contain which vegetables, (was it eight rows of corn last year or six? He'd have to check his notebook) and carved another trio of rows into his carefully leveled soil.

He dragged the plow over the square of garden Joann had tended to for the past four summers. Earlier in the week he'd told her it was ready for her to plant, she'd looked at him with pity, then to her mother who was elbows-deep in a sink-full of dishes. They'd gardened together since she was four, each year squealing at the sight of the first prong of green slicing through the soil, but it seemed to him now she felt she was doing him a favor. He didn't quite understand who his girls were becoming.

Just that previous night his family had gone to Charles and Edna's for dinner, as they'd been doing at least once a month for the past year. As usual, John provided the vegetables: lettuce, tomatoes, kohl rabbi, everything but the beets. A doughy scabbing had infected his entire batch, so when they arrived at Charles and Edna's, Grandpa Chuck asked the girls to help dig some from his garden.

At dinner, Michelle had loaded her plate with beets and nothing else. She scraped their greens into a pile, each leaf with its own screech. Jon had thought it was odd—his daughters had always refused to even try them. No one else seem to notice her plate, each person concerned with slathering butter on the corn, and carving mashed potato caverns for the steaming gravy. Michelle slowly sliced each beet into thirds, then shoved them into her mouth. When she finally looked up from her project, she saw Jon watching her, and she smiled the forced smile she saved to ruin photographs—eyes squinted tightly shut, mouth stretched to reveal as many teeth as possible. The blood from the beets had stained her teeth blue and ran in a slow river from one corner of her mouth.

After dinner, Charles suggested corn field hide-and-go-seek to the girls. Michelle rolled her eyes but grabbed her sister's hand and disappeared into the corn. While Jon was meticulously tidy about his garden, Charles planted things in the spring and hoped for the best. His corn stalks were at least six feet high and the rows crooked and weedy. Jon thought it was creepy as hell—he'd always been sure to make his own corn rows carefully enough to see out from any point, but the girls zipped and weaved through the stalks, appearing to understand the logic of the flawed patterns. Edna even joined in, following Charles with a limp because of a bunion, waddling and lurching to keep up with him. Jon had wrapped his arms around Mary-Ellen and listened to Charles' laughter and the girls' shrieking. Near dusk sent stalk-shadows ten feet high and they stepped into one of them to protect their eyes from the setting sun.

Dwayne Jeffries heard the gunshot while peeling soup labels off his neighbors' aluminum cans. Chicken Noodle was the overwhelming favorite—the occasional Tomato appeared during summer months. Sometimes coupons were printed on the backs of the labels, and he figured the savings part of his wage. He didn't eat these soups—he worried about the effects of too much sodium in one's diet—but he liked to have them on hand in case of visitors. He ate only fresh fruit and vegetables, whole wheat bread, eggs, chicken, and the occasional steak when Jon Williams was cleaning out his freezer to prepare for the fresh meat he turned his cows into. He accepted the organ meat, but slipped it into the burning barrel when Jon was at work. "So fresh, it's still breathing," Jon said when he handed him the heart and liver. "Wife can't stand it in the house or I'd eat it myself." Dwayne wasn't an ungrateful man, but he believed eating heart and liver wasn't good for one's heart or liver.

The gunshot didn't worry him. His body was whole, unwounded, and his father was resting safely in his bed, drooling bits of gummed animal crackers onto the towel tucked into his collar. Buster Jeffries was now in the latter stages of Alzheimer's. Dwayne had first known something was wrong when he walked in on his father urinating onto the wood stove and not showing a hint of surprise at the piss hissing on the surface. Buster had zipped up his trousers, turned to Dwayne and said, "Doesn't anyone knock any goddamned more?"

Dwayne Jeffries knew the neighbors thought he'd been to jail, that he'd been convicted of rape and served five years at Walla Walla State. The oldest Williams girl had told him so week after he'd returned home.

Though Jon Williams had told Dwayne he was "goddamned sorry to hear about your dad," Dwayne knew Jon Williams watched him, and that each bit of action on the Jeffries' property translated into something disgusting, immoral, and illegal. When Dwayne dumped the burnables into his barrel, wedged twisted pages of the *Record Journal* into the spaces the garbage naturally fell into, and lit it, he knew that even in these everyday actions there were things to ponder and fear and talk about with one's wife or neighbor or kids. County folk were actually very poetic, he thought, in their insistence upon metaphor and symbolism; a thing never meant just that thing, but usually a thing entirely more dangerous.

Dwayne didn't blame the neighbors for their assumptions about him. He even took a little pleasure in constructing their translations of the everyday into something they only allowed themselves to think about in the context of his alleged behavior. He understood the complexities of the act of rape. He believed most men imagined rape in a way that most reflected what they most desired. He, too, understood metaphor, and had his own interpretation of what it meant to methodically plant each seed into a garden three times bigger than was needed to feed one's family– Jon's shovel, hoe, spade, and his ridiculous handmade row-maker each served a specific sadistic purpose. And Charles with his barn and its four feet deep pool of loosened hay for the kids to fling their bodies into from various ledges and ladders, laughing hysterically, having no idea how close they'd come to the concrete underneath.

Still, every week Dwayne drove from house to house on his block, picking up carefully labeled and bagged garbage not fit for burning. The pop and beer cans brought a ½ cent per, and his neighbors drank enough of both to easily cover his gas, groceries, and a monthly dinner-and-movie out. He'd been doing this for almost a year now, and though it took some of them awhile to be comfortable with his weekly stops on their property, they appreciated the service–no one enjoyed being responsible for dealing with their own garbage. And Jon and Charles thought every man, no matter his faults, had a right to earn an honest living.

Jon's wife, Mary-Ellen, thought very little about Dwayne and his possible prison past or what might have led him there. She knew the suspicions of her husband and neighbors, each version uniquely grotesque depending on the gossiper. But she left that kind of thing up to Jon to worry about and she trusted in his ability to keep her and the girls safe from those tangible threats. Her job was less literal, and certainly not resolved with something as simple as a gun in the nightstand. She'd been living off Tab and Weight Watcher meals since she'd read *Our Bodies, Ourselves*, and believed there was nothing more important than making the girls understand they were the bosses of their bodies—they had "the say." Her husband often teased her when she cooked the food: "That smells like what I shovel from the barn. I paid how much for that?" But the diet was working—at her last weigh in she was eight pounds under her pre-baby weight. And when she slid into her old jeans and saw no fat slumping over the edges, a thrill zipped through her body into places she hadn't noticed for years. She knew Jon felt the zip too. The sex was similar, but she heard the swish-swosh of mouthwash from the bathroom before he slid into bed, felt the tiny pricks of freshly trimmed pubic hair against her skin.

Her new body was about to have another alteration: she was scheduled to have a hysterectomy in two weeks, and though the thought of surgery made it a little less easy to take a deep breath, part of her was curious about the weight of a uterus. Surely it couldn't be much, but every little bit counted. She was of course looking forward to surgery for medical purposes. She had something her doctor called "Pelvic Adhesions" that caused her a great deal of pain. The doctor explained the condition by saying that the slippery things inside had become sticky. He'd given her some pamphlets to read. She'd looked through them, reading the writing in bold at the beginning of each section, and the next day called to schedule the surgery.

Because Mary-Ellen knew children, especially girls, rarely took the word of their mothers, she used non-verbal techniques to persuade the girls to empower themselves. The girls had no idea they'd been drinking two percent, or that the American cheese on their sandwiches contained just half the fat of the regular slices. She believed they had no idea she knew of the book, *Savage Thrust*, the older girl read then hid in a place obvious enough for the younger to find, read for a bit, and return having taken the care to memorize the page number rather than the tell-tale sign of a dog-eared corner. *Savage Thrust* contained descriptions of acts she certainly didn't want the girls engaging in, but she had been surprised and impressed at how the female characters chose when, where, how, and with whom to please themselves. Jon had always been a generous lover, but it hadn't occurred to her she could have such say and variety in her own pleasure until quite recently. She wasn't naïve enough to assume she could have a conversation about such things with her girls without creating an awkward situation—the book was a blessing.

Michelle knew her mother had found *Savage Thrust*. She saw it smeared all over her mother's body like she felt it on her own. She noticed the jeans her mother was wearing, so tight she would've warned Michelle about damaging her "lady-bits" had Michelle worn them. And the shoes she crammed her toes into while simply working in the house or going shopping for food at the Mark-and-Pack. Michelle noticed the women in the book were always about to be "taken with ferocious abandon," even while they were doing normal things such as vacuuming or fixing a sandwich. The women often resisted, but soon gave in and lost all control.

Michelle had just covered her ears with the hood of her sweatshirt and slipped into Grandpa Chuck's pool of hay when she heard the gunshots. When she was seven she'd jumped into the hay from the second tier, and a blade of hay had entered her ear and stuck into the wax. She'd felt it in her body so deeply that when she pulled it out she was sure some crucial part had been lost. When she woke up every morning she'd try to recall something from each year of her life, just to make sure she still could, then checked the pillow case for some sign of dying. From where she lay now she could see the soles of Christina's shoes dangling from the edge of a bail. She hated Grandpa Chuck's barn–there was something sour in the thick air that coated her throat, but she'd been following Christina for over an hour, and this is where she'd been led.

Michelle had begun following Christina around the neighborhood after she'd noticed her wearing new Levi's; who got new jeans in the middle of the summer? Michelle loved the curved stitch on the pocket, the button-fly that kept the crotch from creeping. She'd wanted a pair for two years, but they weren't the best deal at Sears, and Michelle's father worked too hard to blow his money on a name brand. Christina's body seemed designed for the jeans, curves where Michelle had edges, skin where Michelle had bone.

The gunshot didn't cause Michelle any concern. Someone could've been shooting at a coffee can wedged onto a fence post, "helping" a cat that crawled away from the busy road, hind quarters dragging flat, or slamming two bullets into the brain of the cow that would feed a family for a year. She'd watched her father do all of these things, and even mentally prepared herself for the task of finishing off a cat if the need arose and her father was away. He'd shown her and Joann where to aim to make sure it was "quick and painless."

When Christina stood and Michelle saw the dark stain of urine on those Levi's, Michelle said something she'd been told to never say, and never before been compelled to say.

Christina turned but not toward Michelle. She looked out the window Charles shoved the hay bales onto a conveyer belt from that lowered them to the ground. She looked back toward the batch of kittens, wondering if what her mother said was true about the effects of touching newborn kittens: "Get your smell all over them and their mother may reject them." Some of them were still damp from their mother licking clean the blood and mucous. The mother surely couldn't reject them all, she thought, and she lifted each one individually, cradling each in the palm of her hand, checked the sex then positioned what she thought were the females in front of the mother's nipples.

Moments after the gunshot, Joann found Michelle watching Christina in the barn. Joann had been following Michelle since she'd started refusing to play the games they'd played before—cribbage, Life, even the spy game they'd perfected the summer before. It had been two months since she'd peered into Grandpa Chuck's basement window and seen his head buried between Michelle's legs. Joann had crouched lower in the garden bed, her chin denting the soil behind the rose bush, and focused on the meaty valleys her sister was scratching into her arms.

Joann saw Christina's pants and smelled the urine immediately. She shivered. She herself refused to let any smells to collect on her body. She showered daily, sometimes twice if she could convince her mother she'd spent too much time in the barn or the dog had thrown up on her, and had for the last six months since she'd sat down to pee and saw the blood smeared on her underwear. She wasn't scared or surprised, just disgusted at what her body contained. She had taken off the underwear and scrubbed the crotch down with the Borax soap her father used to clean oil and grease from his hands. She knew her older sister hadn't yet gotten her period; she'd inspected her underwear while doing laundry and saw nothing marring the clean white cotton crotches.

Joann left Michelle to her watching and walked the path to her house. She was sticky and sure she could smell the meaty scent of blood on her body. Her father was in the garden, but didn't look up when she jogged by and into the house. She used to love to garden with him, but now all she could think of was the shit that plopped from the pink asses of the cows that eventually spread over the soil. She couldn't stomach the thought of eating her old favorites: sweet, crunchy carrots, the fat bright tomatoes she used to pop into her mouth and explode between her teeth–seeds spraying like bullets.

In the shower, blood oranged by the water slid down the drain. She dragged a razor against her armpit and legs. Though she'd left it alone up until this point, she shaved the small patch of pubic hair with two swipes of the razor. She'd been nervous to do so thus far—her mother swore that once she started to shave the hair would grow back faster, thicker, darker, but the sleek, clean feel of her legs and armpits was too tempting. She patted herself dry with a towel dark enough to hide any sign of what her body was up to.

Ruby's List

Ruby calls to say she's killed the baby. I spread avocado onto a bagel and say I'm on my way. I hang up, open wide, and take my time chewing. I figure I can get at least half of it down before she calls to hurry me.

She's killed the baby before. And the cat, the neighbor's sheep, the white squirrel that clicked its claws against the back steps, demanding peanuts.

I've killed the baby, too. Everyone had. Suffocated, choked, drowned, electrocuted—we were a violent bunch with a way of just-barely. I wondered why she kept us as friends. Would you socialize with your baby's murderers? But she always called. I'm up to second on her call list. I saw the list the last time I saved the baby. I debuted at number seven, just above Pat the Mortician (he's been removed; she said it was a conflict of interest on his part) and just below Billy the Banker, who lends her money so her checks don't bounce.

Last June, Alison, who'd been at number one for a couple of years, finally told her, I can't do this anymore. You're nuts. Ruby had pounded on her door at four am, screaming, begging, please, the casserole, E. coli, children.

Elizabeth became number one, and I, because I saved the children from the E. coli, number two. Elizabeth was a Christian and had gone to Teens for Christ and Young Life. We hung out with her because she smoked more pot than anyone around. I'm pretty sure she'll stay number one, (the pot makes her really patient and god keeps her in at night) and that I'll mess up number two soon enough. I drink too much to drive at night, sleep too heavily to wake up early. But I am happy to be number two. I don't think I've ever been second on a list of anything.

I met Ruby before the baby died and died and died. She hired me to work at the sub shop even though I wasn't old enough to use the meat slicer. She wore her hair in two braids. Every day after lunch rush, she'd sit in the back of the restaurant, unbraid, brush each side exactly ten times, and whip them into tight new braids.

Sometimes after work we'd go to the bar to play pool. I'd buy $3.00 pitchers of Pabst with my tip money. We'd drink three or four each time, and by eleven I'd be dying to go home with her. I'd ask if she wanted a ride, or wanted to make a pizza or something, but she'd look at me like, come on, we both know what you want.

I sort of agreed, but that didn't stop the wanting, or change the fact we'd slept together a couple weeks after I started working with her. She showed up at my apartment one night. I figured I'd forgotten to lock the door or turn off the ovens at the deli. But she clomped into the living room, straddled my hips and wrapped her arms around my neck.

I poured some wine and she talked about her boyfriend. I'd heard of him before, only briefly, and wasn't all together sure he existed. But she was crying like he must.

She spent a while in the bathroom. I was worried so I knocked. She said, Come in, and there she was, holding the scissors to the base of her braid. I said she shouldn't, she'd regret it, then at least let me help.

In seconds, each braid lay on the floor. She slammed past me and into the kitchen for more wine.

I picked up the braids. I was surprised how heavy they were.

Do you want to keep them? I asked.

She looked at me like I was nuts, like I might ask her next if I should carve out her eyes so she could see what she looked like from over here.

Can we go to bed? She asked.

I didn't think us having sex was the greatest idea for me or her or her boyfriend, but we went to my room right then. She said if we were going to do this, that if I was going to be the "other man," anything goes and I thought of dildos, vibrators, handcuffs instead of what was a good idea. Then she said anything *I* want goes, and I had no idea what that would be, so I just did what I normally do.

I drove her back to her boyfriend's and thought this might be the first and last time I'd see the sun rise. I didn't know her boyfriend very well but I knew she would tell him where she'd been. I wondered about work and her being my boss and if anything would change, but then that it was sort of conceited to think I could change things.

The phone rings—Ruby—the baby is cooing and drooling and seems to be just fine.

Close call, she says.

I think for a second I can finish eating now, but get in the car anyway. Come on, have you ever had your baby almost die? There's post-trauma, there's re-enactment. She'll need somebody to tell: I don't know what I would've done. My baby, the only thing I've got. God, I can't even think about it, and crumple into understanding arms.

I guess there's also a bit of hope of getting some of something from her, even if it's just giving her a back rub or something. When I give her back rubs, she pulls her pants down so I can just see the beginning of her crack and asks me to tickle her palms and the soles of her feet. And I do, and it's pretty much enough. I'm not a greedy person.

In the car I listen to NPR, because Ruby says it's what people who have a lot to say listen to. I said to her once, Can't they get better sound quality? And she said sound quality is a privilege not everyone can afford.

I try to care, but it's so easy not to, and even if I did, what could I do? Wouldn't I sound like pretty much an asshole if I ran around telling people I cared, telling them we should do something about this and do something about that when I really think it's easy to sit back and drink coffee, or red wine, or whatever, and talk about what everyone is or isn't doing but I haven't a fucking clue what anybody should be doing.

I switch off NPR because it's just too much talking. I turn the corner and my passenger door flaps open. I lean to grab it, a long stretch, I drive a Dodge Dart, and slam it before anyone sees, I think. Ruby is the only one who doesn't make fun of my car. She said it's nice and simple and there's nothing wrong with having things that you can work on yourself.

She went to Spain once, and brought me a little sombrero with white dingelberries for my rear-view mirror. She gave it to me after I spent the night. I think she probably bought it for herself or someone else, because I didn't have a car then.

I asked her why for me and she said she loved what I did to her skin when I touched her, that my fingers dripped heat or electricity or something, and I thought that's just about the best thing anyone's ever said to me.

Then she said if she isn't married by thirty, she'll find me wherever I am and marry me.

Now, I know she said that to make me feel good, and it did, you know, that she said it, but marriage? I promised her I'd wait for her too because she kind of made me by promising me in the first place. I'm pretty sure she won't be married by thirty. She's a lot of work. I'm also pretty sure I won't be married at twenty-five. I'm kind of unmotivated when it comes to women, so I guess we'll be getting married in about five years, which means I'll be number one on Ruby's List.

She's waiting at the door with the baby at her breast. I hate the word breast—it reminds me of nurses or bosom or nuns—but when she's nursing I call it a breast so I think of nurses and nuns instead of putting my mouth around her nipple.

She waves at me, says she's made me lunch and thanks so much for coming. I know she's made tuna on Wasa, but I smile anyway. She knows I don't eat any meat and that I can't tell her no. It's her favorite, so who am I to complain?

I see her nipple when she pulls the baby away. It's huge and purple and totally different than when I touched it. She asks me to hold the baby, to check signs and see what I think and asks, do you think we should take her to the hospital?

I'm twenty and trying to finish my G.E.D, and though she's told me more than once she thinks I'm smarter than most, I have no clue if the baby's okay. Ruby asks me questions all the time: Does garlic go bad? Did you hear the top of the salsa pop? Does carbon monoxide smell like cheese? How would you know if a can of tuna carried botulism?

I used to tell her I don't know but she'd say, okay, okay, but what do you think? So now I answer no or yes and understand that I'll be to blame. She thinks everything is lethal. If she watches television while nursing and the baby gets cranky, she thinks "electronical waves" have soaked into her skin and into its mouth. If she uses the gas stove (which she rarely does, everything is very cold when I eat with Ruby) and the baby falls asleep, she's gassed her. If the baby's fussy or sluggish after a bath, Ruby thinks she's boiled her insides with the bathwater.

I say the baby looks fine.

Since the baby came, she mostly kills it. It's kind of a relief to be able to just come to her house to save things, rather than knock on neighbors' doors and ask to check on their pets, call the health department to make sure there have been no E. coli or hepatitis outbreaks.

You know, I didn't used to kill everything, Ruby says.

I know, I say.

Or think I killed everything, she says.

I'm not, I say.

Not what? She asks.

I know, I meant to say, I say.

Lunch is different today. Tuna on bagels.

In high school, she says, I heard a rumor about myself that I had AIDS.

Really? I say, even though I heard the same thing.

Rumor was I got it from a Canadian hockey player named Lavelle. I'd slept with him in the front seat of his car though I didn't really mean to. I was passing time while my friend and another hockey player had sex on the beach.

Her baby seems to like me. She stays quiet and still in my arms. But god, she's ugly. I have no idea how she came from Ruby. She'd named her Doe because she said the baby looked like a deer, which is fine for a deer, but not a baby. She has huge brown eyes that blink at you when you say Doe, which is pretty cute, but still.

Ruby says, After two weeks of having that feeling in my stomach like when you lose your step at the top of a flight of stairs or almost drive into a tree or ditch, I called Lavelle, reminded him who I was, asked if he had AIDS.

That's ballsy, I say.

He said, No, do you?

A relief, huh? I say.

Yeah, I guess. Although things were rough for a while because during the two weeks I called every guy I'd slept with and told him I had AIDS and he'd better get tested.

That's stupid, I say, then feel like an ass for saying it.

She says, I think I may have even started the rumor.

She takes the baby and tells me to eat. A lot of vegetarians think tuna is the gateway meat before the full on, balls out need for steak and bacon and ribs. I have to be careful. Ruby eats more tuna than anyone I know. Once I saw her garbage full of tin cans and thought she'd probably consumed an entire dolphin by now.

She's wearing her house robe. Ruby is amazing when she's out—lots of layers and the under-layers always match her shoes or hat or tights and the outer layers match each other. Everything looks like it's exactly in the right place. But at home it's always the robe.

I realize she's sitting and not talking or eating and not looking at Doe or me. Where are you? I think of asking her, but I don't because sometimes when she starts she never stops.

Ruby says, I dreamt you saved my life last night. A man in a white suit with a green patch that said Sully's came to my door.

I let him in when he said he had to fix the piping. I was on the phone with you, about the baby, I guess, and he was clanking in the background. You asked what he was doing and I told you he was clanking a fork, knife and spoon together. The clanking was weird to me in the dream, but mostly it was distracting. You told me to run, get out, he was going to kill me. So I pushed him and ran out and screamed for help and you were there.

Creepy, I say.

You said the papers called him "The Cutlery Killer," and that he killed and mutilated women with their own silverware. All I could think about was a fork mixing my guts and scraping my rib. That must be the worst thing imaginable.

But you lived? He didn't get you? I ask.

No, I lived.

I take a small bite. I'm having a hard time swallowing the meat.

A razor blade slicing an eyeball. That's the worst thing I can imagine, I say to make her feel better.

Yeah, that's bad, she says, and she's away again.

Or swallowing a mouthful of glass, I say.

I heard a story about a man raping and killing this girl when I was in middle school. He tore her nipples off with pliers. That's probably worse than the fork thing.

I guess it would be, I say.

I crumple a napkin over the rest of my bagel.

Doe is sleeping in Ruby's arms, her face nuzzled into Ruby's stomach. She's staring at Doe, or actually sort of through her.

My nipples feel like they've been ripped off, she says.

I laugh. She doesn't.

They're cracking and peeling and bleeding. It's disgusting.

Really? I say.

Sometimes I'm afraid I'll accidentally turn too quickly or I'll hear something that makes me jump when I'm in the shower shaving my arm pits and I'll shave and nipple off.

That's really bad, I say.

They must bleed forever, she says.

She has a dishrag thrown over her shoulder like my mom would. It's for Doe, but I hate it when Ruby reminds me of my mother. Or of a mother. It seems so fake, like when you walk into a room and someone's doing something they think makes them look cool or sexy and they know you're there but they act like they don't and keep doing what they're doing and act surprised when you ask what they're doing. When she was pregnant it was weird too—like she was wearing someone else's body.

I wonder what it would look like, she says.

I wonder the same thing, and if the milk would leak out with the blood, but don't say anything. Bloody milk is a terrible thing to imagine.

I keep finding brown stringy pieces in the tuna that Ruby swears aren't worms. I have gum that would help with the taste, but Ruby might get insulted.

Doe seems to be doing fine. I think I'm going to go, I say.

I'm usually dying for Ruby to find a reason or something for me to do so she'll ask me to stay, but I grab my keys.

Doe whimpers, growls, kicks her feet.

Ruby is beautiful now, if I don't look at Doe or the dishrag or think of bloody nipples. Beautiful from the neck up.

Sometimes I think marrying her wouldn't be so bad. I mean, it's not as if I can do any better. I'd have to save everything all the time, I know, but she's pretty much it.

Doe whimpers again, and turns her face away from Ruby.

I'm going to go now, okay? I got things to do, I say.

Yeah, okay, she says.

Why am I going? I don't have anything to do. But the baby's starting to fuss and Ruby's in a way I don't think I can save.

Have I hurt you? she asks.

When? I ask.

Ever, she says.

What do you mean? I say.

I just feel like I must've hurt you at some point. But you never seem hurt, she says.

You haven't, I say.

Never? I mean, I've never really considered it before, she says.

You haven't, I say.

I don't know why I never have, she says.

I wonder why I haven't felt like shit because of her. I mean, I didn't like to think of her with other guys, or see her sitting on their laps or anything, but it never really hurt. It never made me feel like yelling at her or throwing a punch.

Are you okay? I say.

Are you okay? she says.

Yeah, but I need to take off, I say.

Me too, she says. I've been so lightheaded lately.

Ruby's arms stretch toward me, Doe stuck to the ends of them. Ruby says, Will you take her?

I reach for Doe because it looks like Ruby's going to drop her.

I don't want her, she says. Please take her.

What do you mean? I ask. I'm holding Doe but only enough to not drop her. Doe blinks.

Ruby looks very sad and over it at the same time.

I don't want her. I think that's why I always almost kill her, she says.

You never almost kill her, Ruby, I say.

You know that's not true, she says.

For a second I remember I've sort of wondered.

Please, she says, just take her.

Why me? I don't know how to take care of her, I say.

Who else? she says.

I could drop Doe in her playpen and leave. Ruby can't expect me to leave with Doe and not come back. And besides, Doe can't ride in my car. There are no seatbelts and the brakes are shitty and I don't have anything a baby needs.

Ruby's putting milk bottles into a paper bag. The dishrag is on the floor. She takes off her robe. Underneath she's summer-dressed, and paler than I remember. Almost transparent.

Doe is smiling and blinking at me.

Ruby clanks the bag of bottles on the table in front of me.

I'm not taking her, Ruby. I can't take care of a baby.

I'll go then, she says. Everything she needs is in the bag.

Ruby grabs her coat and keys and slams the door. Doe starts to cry and I tell her everything is okay. I put her in her playpen and turn on the TV. I don't care if Ruby doesn't let her watch it. I consider calling Elizabeth, this seems like a situation for a number one friend, but there's a show on I like and Doe has stopped crying.

The Worse You Feel the Better

Annaliese

Because of the way the mind wants to translate the horrible into the benign, I thought I was looking at a strangely limbed tree, perhaps one struck by some sort of disease that caused its bark to waste away and bare its fleshy sapwood. That thought stayed for a second or two, before a gust spread a scent that made nausea surge from my stomach to the backs of my eyes. I stayed at the bottom of a breath and just felt it: my OB had told me to be grateful I felt so terrible, that it meant that everything was doing what it was supposed to. She'd said, "the worse you feel the better." I inhaled, imagined the breath meandering into the depths of my lungs, swishing out the old and useless air, easing the stitches of worry between my ribs, and exhaled. I moved a little closer to the tree, an action which surprised me even as I lifted my foot up and over a rotted tree trunk.

It was only a few steps before I deciphered the bared arms and legs of a man, wrists and ankles tied to twin trees with rope. He was naked except for a pair of white boxer shorts, which were stained with blood and shit and urine. His clothing was to the right of his body, clearly not arranged by a woman. The navy pants were folded zipper out, the pale yellow shirt, arms folded toward the chest. The back of the shirt was stained with a slim smear of dirt, almost as a child had traced its finger down its father's back. Why navy and yellow? Who put it together— would a man think of matching such colors? What kind of man wears a shirt the color of a buttercup? I'd read an article once on the psychology of color choice, but couldn't remember the specifics. Brown leather shoes sat on top of the shirt. The state of the man's clothing and shoes would be of some interest to the police, investigators, the man's loved ones.

The wind blew and the man bobbed and the branches creaked and it occurred to me that he might still be alive. I should focus on the relevant details, the immediate concerns. I might have to save a life today. For a second I couldn't remember exactly where I was, but I heard the grumbling of a truck slowing for the corner where I'd seen people set up signs and blow bubbles and whistles to support the athletes in the Mountains to Molehills relay race. I felt a throb in the back of my throat and thought to step backwards over the branch and continue my walk. I circled my palm over on stomach, or womb, as my husband now referred to it. How would anyone ever know I had been there? When the news broke, I would act shocked at the headlines, receive and make calls and say thank God it wasn't me who found him, after all, only a short walk from home, and what with all that walking I do now.

I kneeled down, my low back under a constant pressure only relieved by doing so, and tightened the muscles that hadn't been strong enough to keep the first baby in. I felt the spread of wetness on my underwear I once would've feared was blood. But I learned to notice the subtle differences in weight and consistency and texture of what my body released after I'd driven to Dr. Flora's, blood soaking the towel wedged between my legs.

I rose slowly with my head still and eyes fixed on his face. His eyes were closed, which again made me think he might be alive, and I noticed he was attractive. He resembled a teacher I'd had as a teenager, a man whose presence had sent my body buzzing. I'd learned, from this teacher's class, about some of the physics of attraction. I remembered his smell, the real one, under the others he used to cover it, and imagined that scent zipping through my nostrils and into my brain and electrifying my most animal places. I was an age that would make our mating legal yet frowned upon by school policy, but how can anyone really deny the complex rules of attraction that lay dormant until the moment we breathe the air of the perfect biological match?

The man in the tree wasn't the teacher. I'd known that as soon as I'd noticed the resemblance. I moved closer to look for a wallet. The wind shivered his hair a bit, and I realized then it wasn't his body producing the smell. Maybe a dead deer or raccoon. I unfolded his navy trousers and slipped my hand in the back pocket and pulled out his wallet. William David Johnson.

William

Though I fought against the men as they twisted my arms and legs behind my back, when I heard the zip of the ties around my ankles and wrists, I relaxed and waited. I heard the thud of the bat and could tell my kneecap had split; I saw the flash before the floodlight split the thin meat of my forehead. I tasted the familiar tang of blood, and smelled the bodily fluids these actions forced my body to expel. I could tell that these men had never done something like this by the moment of hesitation before each hit, the way they looked to one another, hoping the other would be the one to lose all control and finish me off. After the beating they untied me and took off my shoes and shirt and pants. I could hear them talking, but not their words, and waited for them to tear off my underwear and destroy that which had destroyed so many others, but when I came to, my underwear was on and I was still intact.

I didn't mean to be who I was. It was only weeks after the first explosion of a wet dream woke me that I walked in on my sister in the bath, unzipped my jeans, grabbed her long black hair, slick with shampoo, and pulled her face into my crotch. The bubbles from the shampoo slid down the back of my hand and I could smell their scent for the rest of the day. I didn't know what I was doing, but she seemed to, and it was done quickly. Afterward, I smacked her forehead into the edge of the tub before I knew I had done it. She wept and moaned in her room for hours, telling my parents she had a terrible headache, maybe even a migraine. At my mother's request, I brought my sister a hot water bottle for her to curl around, an ice pack for her head. My mother believed most unpleasant conditions were easily remedied. When I lay the ice pack over her forehead, I told her I was sorry for her headache. And I was. I'd never planned on giving her a headache.

The men had interrupted me on duty, which is what I called it even though I knew the actual term was grooming. There were two girls collecting sticks and arranging them into some sort of shelter. From the first look, it wasn't clear which one would be a better choice. Not only for my own benefit, but also for hers. I'm not a monster. I looked for the one that already wore the slouch so obvious on girls that have been chosen by people like me. The damage was already done, and they were generally easier to convince to keep quiet and knew what to do.

I'd heard the men approach, and stood to face them. I had nothing to hide yet. But I looked at one man and saw he had eyes so light the looking into them made mine water, the same eyes of the girl I'd weeks earlier talked into my car, a ride home, yes, I live really close to you, know your folks, it's getting pretty dark, sweetie, isn't it? It didn't make it any easier to resist when it required so little creativity or persuasion. It was always so easy to get them to do what I wanted.

I hadn't actually done all I'd wanted to her. Though the girl with the light eyes looked so perfect from my car, so young and sweet kicking up water in the creek, splashing her friend, kneeling now and then to search for a tadpole, her sneaky scoop of water to try to catch one, her body was more developed than I'd thought, thick hair where I preferred soft down, a fullness of the skin I preferred taut. I made do, as they say, but was left with more frustration than satisfaction.

The wind blew across my lips, and I could tell the cracks had set in. When I licked them my jaw clunked and I sensed the pressure pinching in the deepest part of my ear. There was something so easy about this licking, and I realized my front teeth were gone.

I opened my eyes to the ground to look for my teeth, and saw my clothes folded under my feet. I thought the teeth might be under the clothes, or scattered in the leaves and mud, or perhaps even tucked into my pocket the way a mother would tuck lunch money. I moved my tongue over the bloody sockets and remembered rubbing my thumb over the swollen gums in my daughter's mouth. There was a sweetness to an infant's breath when they teethe unlike any other scent: intimate, one-of-a-kind. I suspect only a biological parent could identify it from that of another infant. Her fussy twisting and moaning had calmed when I had done this, her tiny hand grasped my wrist as if to say please don't stop.

Should I have fought harder to live and be a father longer? My daughter only had four teeth, so many more to come and go. I'd been able to comfort her in a way her mother hadn't—who would soothe the swelling before the eruption of the other teeth? Who knows how happy I could've made her, at least for a while. Even with my sister there was a life before when we laughed and played. When we raced, each desperate to be the first to stomp tracks through a batch of fresh snow or find the first ripe tomato. Played war, old maid, cribbage. When, because it saddened her, I pierced the worm with the hook just below what we imagined its neck and cinched its body into that J shape, and then, because it disgusted me, she slit open the just-caught fish and made it dinner. When we wrestled like kittens playing, only to giggle and gasp and exhaust ourselves with laughter. There was that time, I'm sure of it. Perhaps I could've loved my daughter as a proper father, taught her to feel secure and trusting of men, then left before she became something I couldn't stop myself from destroying.

Edward

There are just some goddamned things you cannot control. Like when it didn't rain that summer for four months and there was a mandatory NO WATERING ordinance and my entire garden, with the exception of the tomatoes, which tended to thrive under stress, went to shit. We had to eat store-bought corn, beans, and carrots for months. The Jeromes, Goddamn bless them, shared their peas and potatoes with us that year. Thank Jesus for neighbors that understand what's important, that look out for you and yours like their own. Probably sounds sick that I can go on about things like peas and carrots and corn and beans after doing what I did. I won't deny that. No matter what I did the damage can't be undone, and I know that good as anyone. But things can be done to make sure no one else will wish to hell it was otherwise.

My daughter didn't think I could tell what'd happened to her, but I knew it the way I knew the ripeness of a cob of corn without even touching it. She didn't do any of the normal things you'd expect a little girl to do. She didn't curl up to her mama and not let go, or twitch or wince when I hugged her. But it was still all over her the way a just-butchered cow's smell seeps into your clothes and skin and won't wash out. But it was easy to see she walked a little different, like someone who's trying not to slip. I asked her mother if she thought something was up with her, a mother knows that sort of thing, right? But she said that was how girls act when they are becoming women. I said, She's eleven, what kind of woman could she be, and my wife said, Fathers never know when their baby girls become women.

I had stuffed an oil rag into his mouth and duct-taped it. I couldn't stand the thought of him being able to beg for mercy or to pray to God. Killing him was so much easier than I'd expected. He didn't even flinch when I swung the bat at his head. Or kick or cry or scream when my neighbor shattered his kneecaps and kicked out his teeth, both things I'd never have done myself. I didn't want to make him suffer. He didn't deserve to be a victim. He just deserved to be done.

I remember that when my wife was pregnant with our daughter, someone told me having a kid was like living life with your heart outside your body. Well, that isn't really true. It's more like living with your heart and your lungs and your brain and your guts and your liver and your spleen and any other organ meant for the inside on the out, exposed to the whim of anyone out there that has things they can't stop themselves from doing. Or can stop, but don't. When I got home, changed out of my coveralls, took a shower, and Knocked-Before-Entering like the sign on her door requested, I told her, Honey, that man will never hurt you again. She looked at me and her eyes were big and wet like Bossie's had been the second after the bullet slammed into her brain, almost like she knew that soon enough she'd be hanging in the barn, her guts and blood and shit pooling on the big blue butcher tarp.

Like I said, there are some things you just cannot control. But there are things you can, and you sure as hell better.

William

I saw the woman walking toward me, and I thought, for a split second, that my mother was coming to save me as she had so many times before. Perhaps it is a function of basic biology—a chemical reaction to think of one's mother as death is approaching. I couldn't separate hearing from sight, so I only heard the sound of her approaching when my eyes were open. She stopped and looked up at me, then I blinked and there was only darkness and silence. My mother had once caught me with my sister. I'd waited in her closet until my sister had crawled into bed, then opened the door slowly, growling quietly. I'd only planned to startle her—we were still children and sometimes I just wanted to play games with her like we'd always done—scare her half to death then fall down giggling, promising, Sorry, Sorry, but the look on your face, but she was watching me from her bed, no fear in her eyes, just watching.

I knew you were there, she said. You don't scare me.

I was on top of her in an instant. I held a pillow over her face and yanked up her nightgown. She lay completely still. I was off her by the time my mother opened the bedroom door, but was still holding the pillow over her face. My mother came to me, took my hand and said, Poor Willy, sleepwalking again, and led me to my bedroom.

There were only a few more times after that. Each time I hurt her in a way I didn't mean to: bruises, scratches, bumps, blood. I was always sorry about that. My sister's body soon began swelling and growing hair, her actions more intentional and contemplative, and I lost all interest. Sometimes I'd suggest a game of rummy or cribbage and she'd oblige, but there was never anything in her eyes or her voice that suggested she was anything other than destroyed.

I saw the woman reach into the pocket of my slacks, and I thought to ask about my teeth. She didn't appear to be scared. How did she know the men who did this to me weren't nearby? I heard from my mother that my sister had become a wonderful woman. Successful, happy, and healthy. I wondered how that was possible; could it be what I did wasn't what I remembered? That I'd overestimated my own effect on others?

The woman stood and stepped back from my things. She rubbed her stomach the way I'd seen my wife do when she was pregnant. She didn't look far along, perhaps a four or five months, just far enough to want a girl, but pray for a boy.

Annaliese

I looked at his license. He was smiling in the picture and I thought again how attractive he was. Someone must be missing him. A woman I'd had a college class with went missing on a hike not far from here. At our professor's encouragement we'd distributed flyers around campus and held a vigil that packed the center of campus and drew in so many people that the light from our candles made the whole world seem on fire. A friend of hers had spoken that night, asking us to be silent to look into every face we could see from where we stood and understand how many people this woman mattered to. Later I'd learned there were over a thousand faces there, a thousand people missing one, a thousand lives undone, at least a little, by this one missing.

Months later I'd dreamed I'd killed that classmate. That I'd smashed her head in with a rock, over and over until her face lay like lasagna in her skull. I had no idea why I'd dreamed this; I liked this woman, she was kind, intelligent, friendly, happy. I continued to see flashes of what I'd done during the seconds between sleep and wakefulness, in that time when it is so difficult to tell what is real and what is not, and then for weeks later. When her body was found and cause of death revealed as a self-inflicted gunshot wound to the head I felt relief. It was horrible. Tragic. Heartbreaking. But it was her choice.

I slid the license into the wallet, and saw a flash of color from the cash pocket. I pulled out a stack of photos, the one on top an infant in a baptismal dress, and then photo after photo of different girls, all nine or ten or so. It was clear William David hadn't made the choice to die here. But he must've made choice after choice that led to this place. We have choices to make about how much suffering we can stand, and how much we allow others to suffer.

Though my husband had pleaded with me not to, I'd held my dead daughter before I let them take her. My husband hadn't even wanted to see her, but I couldn't let her be gone without knowing if she favored me or my husband, if she had that strange thumb that runs on my side, or the attached earlobes on his. Most would be surprised at how developed a 13-week fetus was—fingernails, eyebrows, wrinkles where the fingers bend. She wore an expression I recognized as one of my husband's. I'd seen the expression on him only a few times, when he'd heard the results of his younger brother's finally-clear CAT scan, when he'd learned I was pregnant after two years of trying, and again during our eight week ultra sound, telling us we had a viable fetus.

I stared at her and waited for the sight of her to tear my heart out. I didn't feel anything in my heart, but instead the entire length of my spine throbbed. So this is what death feels like, I'd thought. I raised the bundle toward my husband, it was like lifting a handful of leaves, but he waved his hands and reached for the door. I considered dropping her. He'd have to catch her, wouldn't he? He couldn't just let her fall. I said to my husband, "hold her, you fucking coward."

The sky was darker now, and William David was starting to look more like a shadow than a person. I considered looking for his missing teeth—surely someone would be comforted by them being buried with his body. We buried our baby's ashes five days ago. We'd kept them in her nursery for months, but once I found out I was pregnant again I knew we had to let her go. Her ashes had fit in a box the size of one of those miniature cereal boxes that had always caused me such disappointment— never enough and always the plainest kinds, Corn Flakes, Raisin Bran, instead of Cookie Crisp or Honey Combs.

During the burial, my husband had stood behind me, arms wrapped gently around my stomach, face wedged between my neck and coat. In bed that night he'd lifted the blankets and pressed his mouth to my stomach. He'd done this often during the first pregnancy, to say, Hello, baby, We love you, We can't wait to meet you. I put my hand on his head, remembering, as my mother had told me, he was suffering too. He moved his lips over my bellybutton and whispered, You wouldn't be here if she hadn't died. Don't ever forget that.

I had covered my stomach and rolled away and imagined positive, healthy energy being sent from my brain to the baby like I'd read in my keeping-a-pregnancy books. I waited for him to wedge his knees into the back of mine and wrap his arm around my belly, but his chalky snore came quickly, and the space between us was filled by our needy cat.

On my walk home I prepared myself to be destroyed while telling the story of the hanging man, first on the phone to 911, then to my husband. I'd schedule the abortion for as soon as possible. No one would ever have to know this undoing was my doing; who wouldn't miscarry after witnessing such horror? The details of the hours before William's death would surely come out and people would come forward and the kind of man he was would be made clear. And his mother, perhaps, would weep in front of the camera, swear he'd been such a good boy, how could anyone do something like this to her boy, and I would cry about my loss, all of it so unfair, destroyed again to all those around me, but with a heart as light as leaves.

What the Blood Tells You to Be

The morning after I found the boys masturbating, I slid three sunny-side up eggs onto each of their plates, sliced toast into strips they would dip into the yolks. They ate as usual, saving the final strip of toast to drag around their plates in a slow circle. I couldn't shake my expectation they should be embarrassed at what I'd walked in on, though there was no reason they would. They had been saved from the corruption and temptation of the outside world, and had no concept of what one should and should not do in the presence of others. As I rinsed the yolky smears from their plates, hair stood erect on my skin, and thought I might have to go to the toilet to relieve the boiling in my stomach. I knew the day would come when I would no longer be able to ignore the bodies of my boys becoming those of men. I'd heard their voices stumble into deeper octaves, noticed them fingering the wispy hair on their upper lips. They had begun to understand what it was their bodies were programmed to do millions of years ago, and they would soon be capable of anything to get it done. There is such burden that accompanies preparing boys for the world—the men they will become possess such deeply encoded abilities to destroy.

Up until that morning I had no doubt I was the best person to teach the boys anything they needed to know, but the eruption in my gut insisted it was time to enlist the help of another. I found Everett two weeks later when he responded to an ad I placed: "Homeschooling Family Seeking Biology Tutor." I offered $150 an hour, plus gas, and reviewed over forty responses before I found Everett's. He was the only one that had included a photo, as well as offered to do any kind of screening I felt appropriate. At the interview, I told him the boys had a condition that made them extremely susceptible to infection and disease, which made homeschooling and isolation necessary. The condition, I told him, often cleared up at adulthood, and I expressed hope the boys would one day lead a normal life. Only the last bit of that statement was true, a normal life, but I shared some photos of inflamed skin rashes, boils, even warts I claimed were from the boys' bodies. I lamented upon the pain they endured, flipping each photo over and stating, *They were only three here, can you imagine?*

When he left, he mentioned my bravery and strength, and I let the compliment in and felt heat spread across my cheeks. The truth of my situation was far worse, far more challenging and perilous than an unsightly skin infection. I couldn't remember the last time someone had complimented me on anything. I'm not ignorant of the strangeness of my circumstances. I am only doing what I feel is right for our family, and for the well-being of others. Isn't that all we can be expected to do?

Today will be Everett's first day. Though it is difficult to find others who understand the way things must be for our family, he seems a good fit, and he has signed a lengthy contract that details what the boys must not be exposed to: television, music, computers, magazines, t-shirts with words printed across them. In addition to more traditional teachings about physiology and biology, Everett's job will be to help me assess the boys' ability to become members of a society to which they will contribute, not destroy.

After the boys bathe and eat, they stomp outside to collect eggs and feed and run the dogs. Their heavy boots clomp down the cedar porch stairs as my slippered feet pad up the carpeted ones to my room. During breakfast, an image of Everett sent a throb between my legs and I had to cross them to contain the pressure. While I rinsed the dishes, I hunched and opened my shoulders so the material of my nightgown could brush against my nipples. Though I had already done so upon waking, my body tells me I must alleviate before Everett arrives in an hour. I can't risk distracting him.

I alleviate in the shower and drape a loose dress over my body. *It is more a curse than a gift to have a body like yours,* my mother used to say. It took me two years of my brother's visits, as he called them, for me to be able to fully ignore the weight of his body on mine, parts of him in parts of me, and the hot wetness of his breath on whatever part of my body he breathed on. I remember that first time of freedom—I was fourteen and he sixteen, and though I clearly heard him enter my room and felt the mattress dip from his weight, there was nothing else that filled that time as far as I could recall. When he opened my bedroom door to leave, he looked back at me to say goodnight, and I thought I'd been dreaming for lack of memory of his visit until the semen leaked from my body onto the sheets.

He only visited a few times after that, each time I was left with no memory beyond his entrance and exit. I knew even then the incredible feat I'd achieved: the power to forget, to essentially control the actions of those who put upon me because of the ability to erase all but the physical evidence of them.

Downstairs the boys are rinsing three dozen eggs, and I can smell the dogs on their clothes and hair.

"How much longer?" Adrian asks. It would be a shame for another to never run their fingers through his curls, or to feel the heat his body could generate in theirs.

"Very soon."

Charly lifts the last of the eggs from the wash, pats it dry with a towel and places it in the carton. He does this as he has been taught, but he also handles most objects like eggs, cradles toys and rocks and balls as if they are forced to contain something precious with inadequate exteriors.

"He's here!" Adrian calls from the front door, already unlatching the lock and stepping back to let the door swing wide.

And indeed he is. Everett's boot emerges from behind his car door, the rest of him rising as if in water. I can smell him before he steps through the doorway—a salty smell that hits me between the eyes and pricks my skin warm. Aside from his interview, which was conducted in a café along the highway full of people going elsewhere, it has been years since I have been this close to a man and I have little ability to resist thoughts of what my body wants me to do to him.

"Welcome, Everett. You should have everything you need in the dining room. I'll be upstairs out of your way."

His Yes, Ma'am is absorbed by the folds of my frumpy dress. My mind is already set on alleviation. It is very difficult to resist thoughts from conjuring while I do it, but my will is good and I manage a purely individual experience that relies only on the sensations I can provide myself.

When Everett's two hours are up, I enter the kitchen.

"Coffee, Everett?"

Charly looks just to the left me when I ask how things went. The boys are electric with knowledge. Adrian's chest seems broader and he walks more heel toe, heel toe, excited by the possible functions of his body but a little shocked as to why.

The boys grab their sandwiches from the refrigerator and scatter. They have free time until 1:30, and I do my best not to monitor it too closely. They are aware that others exist in the world, but our land stretches over twenty acres, so I trust they won't meet with any unexpecteds. They believe every family lives like this until children reach a certain point where they venture out. For now, they seem content.

"Would you like some coffee, Everett?" I repeat. He is shuffling through papers, tucking the boys' worksheets into their folders.

"Of course, ma'am," he says.

Everett speaks in bursts between the tinny racket of the coffee grinder. How have you been, ma'am, Thank you again for this opportunity, ma'am, Is there anything else I can do for you today? I serve him coffee, black as requested, while I fill mine a quarter with the rich cream skimmed from the top of the milk. I've noticed more bone than curve lately, and the tendons in my neck bulge unsightly from certain expressions. I lift down the butter rolls from the top of the refrigerator.

"If I leave them out they'd be gone in an hour."

I serve us each a butter roll and set out more butter to slather on mine. I can feel him watching me, certainly wondering how I can eat like this and look like I do.

"Would you like to take some eggs?" I nod toward the eggs drying in the rack. "We can spare a dozen or so at least."

Everett looks toward the eggs and pauses. There was a time that I would've filled the pause with chatter, avoided silence at all cost, but that is a me of former days. While he's looking at the eggs I study him. From a recent physiology unit with the boys, I recognize the slope of the trapezius as it descends into the deltoid, the rise and fall of the pectoris as it rides the curve of his breath. Only two hours have passed since I alleviated, but I feel a tapping and shift in my chair.

"I could take a half dozen. Any more would go to waste and I'd hate to have that on my conscious." He smiles when he says this, but his words are heavy with throat.

I move to the bin and saw a carton in half. I pick out all white and light brown eggs, and only those no larger than medium to avoid anomalies. There is an embarrassment that comes along with the opulence of double-yolked egg which occasionally occurs in the large eggs. The first time I saw one I literally gasped, and for the rest of the day like I'd caught someone in a private moment.

Everett is behind me the second I fold the carton's tab into the groove. I breathe deeply, letting his scent replace the stale air that has settled at the bottom of my lungs. Sometimes imagine I can breathe in enough of someone that I can become them, or at least a little less me. I'd first imagined this when I breathed in the air of the boys while I held them on my chest, gently rubbing the vernix into their skin while their lips and tongue learned the language of my nipples.

"I hope you enjoy the eggs. They are as fresh as they come."

"Yes, ma'am."

Thursday night is the boys' night to cook dinner and I have made a private oath to never complain about their culinary skills. Adrian fries pork chops in one pan and ground sausage in another. From the living room (where I sit to dissuade an urge for commentary) I can hear the staticky slurp of fat from pan to baster, then its sneeze into the sink. I think to remind them to run hot water to clear the drain and then the water hisses on. Good boys. My only request for these meals is that they include at least one vegetable other than a potato, and I hear a rhythmic thump of knife against cutting board—carrots? Beets?

At dinner, the boys saw into their chops and crumble sausage patties over mounds of potatoes. Stalks of broccoli lay untouched on each plate; they will only eat it after they are full so it doesn't ruin their hunger.

"The middle one, probably," Adrian says between bites. "Or maybe the one on the left."

Charly looks at me but I focus on my broccoli, separating each spear as if there was a reason to do so.

"How can you not know? How can it be either one or the other? Just choose," Charly says. "I chose right away."

The dishwasher chugs and gurgles in the kitchen. I'm certain it is only half full; they understand the importance of cleanliness but not the need to protect essential resources.

"I guess the one in the middle, then, if I have to choose just one. Do we have to?"

"He said to choose one. Just do it."

They don't know the reasons I've chosen each of the photos Everett showed them. I instructed Everett to tell them to look at each photo and let their body's reaction determine one to choose. The photos are of average looking females. Never would they be referred to as unattractive, but also unlikely to incite intense desire. There is such danger in unreal expectations, and such devastation attached to the assumption of tenderness.

After they finish with the clean-up I will clean up in the morning, I wish them goodnight. I have only alleviated three times today, and if I don't once or twice more my brother will visit in a nightmare.

The week passes as expected; the boys quickly return to their usual behavior, really still children at their core, emotions and actions easily replaced by others. The lesson plan for their second Thursday with Everett goes far beyond anatomy. The boys are to have chosen a photo to present to Everett, and this week the headshots will be reunited with their bodies. They will be instructed to look carefully at the photo and write in their journals anything they notice about the bodies of their chosen photo as well as their own.

When Everett arrives he is carrying a white paper bag. He appears even more attractive this week: a shadow of stubble contours his jaw. He wears similar clothing: a black button up shirt, sleeves rolled just above the elbows, dark jeans over brown boots. In preparation for his arrival, I skipped sitting with the boys for breakfast and alleviated twice, again resisting the manifestation of him in my thoughts, visualizing only the flare of nerve endings and the rush oxytocin into the blood.

"These are for you and the boys." Everett passes me the white bag. Inside, three fat éclairs lay side by side. One of them has been crushed and its creamy filling exposed.

I thank him, set out plates, and cut the damaged eclair into two. My mother raised me to believe that one should always share offerings with the offerer. He eats the éclair in two bites, strings of saliva tethers between it and his mouth while I lift a triangle to my mouth with a fork. Two beads of custard collect on the whiskers of his chin and I resist reaching over and wiping them away.

The boys enter the kitchen with their chosen photos pinched between their fingers. I clear the plates away and leave them to their studies.

I know better than to assume I know which photos they've chosen or about what they've written. I'm not foolish enough to believe I understand them very well at all. Sometimes I look at them and wonder when I will finally accept that they are not mine at all, even though I birthed them and raised them every moment of their lives.

It goes without saying that a mother will do almost anything to protect her children. My mother understood this, and tried to protect me from the actions of my brother; I must believe this to be true. Her only failing was being unwilling to accept the lengths she had to go to. I am without that particular fault.

In my bedroom I unlock my armoire and pull down the box with my brother's ashes to keep me from fixating on Everett. I hold the shirt my brother wore to my wedding—its pattern is so intricate its tiny red and blue paisleys almost appear to be in motion. He stood in photo after photo with me and my new husband— he was the best man and best friend of my husband. At first I let the memories and emotions surface, I wiggle into them until I feel their weight on my skin and sink into them for a moment. Once deep enough, I think to press (not shove, this cannot be done with anger or hatred) them to the outer regions of my brain, away from any hub of emotion, from the deepest core that tells you to rage and resist at all cost.

As I'd hoped, this process exhausts me, and I sleep without realizing it until Charly's tentative knock and voice wakes me.

"I'll be right down, Charly. Ask Everett to wait."

I smooth the wrinkles of sleep from my dress and rub lotion on my face and elbows. The boys are outside running the dogs when I get downstairs. Everett has slipped their chosen photos and written work into a manila envelope.

"They are good boys. I enjoy working with them."

I take the envelope from his hands. Though the beads of custard are gone from his beard, a sweet smell coats my nose and throat.

"Thank you. They seem too good to be true, don't they?" I say.

He agrees, and stands. He stretches his arms above his head, and the strip of skin above his jeans is exposed. I feel my body slam against itself, then retreat into throb. It has been so long since I've seen the body of a man. He finishes the stretch and is again covered.

"The eggs were great. I made an omelet."

The sloppy and remedial use of the eggs interrupts the buzzing from the sight of his skin. Well-fed and cared for chickens produce yokes so vibrant—paling them with their whites seems such a shame.

"Until next week. And thanks again for the éclairs."

After Everett leaves, I set to shucking, blanching, and cutting corn from over one hundred cobs to freeze and feed us far into spring. They boys have done their part by carefully assessing each cob on the stalk for the ideal ripeness—I've shown them the clutch at the base and slow ascension toward the crinkled silk sprouting form the head, so each ear I rip open is perfect. It takes hours to finish and by the time the last bags are properly spaced in the freezer my feet are pounding, so I lay on the couch and raise them. I hold the envelope on my chest and try to force myself to, for once, intuit. I feel the cramp of my organs processing the éclairs and will the fat to settle on my hips, breasts, buttocks, thighs. The pictures of the girls flash and swarm in my mind, but there is nothing that brings forth one or the other. I understand my boys no more than a stranger.

I wake to the sizzle of sausage and onions. There is a procession of clank and thud and scrape and soon a call from the boys that dinner is ready.

"I'll be right there," I say. The envelope and its contents will have to wait.

My senses were wrong—they've actually made a vegetable stir fry with peppers and beans and squash from the garden. Globes of rice, usually only used to hold together a meaty casserole, have been scooped onto each plate. A slab of pink salmon steams in the center of the table.

"We thought you might like something different, mom," Adrian says. He holds the dish with the vegetables above his plate as though he's unsure of what to do with it.

They've never had salmon—Everett must've brought it— and while the pink meat slowly dissolves in my mouth they shove in bite after bite.

"Why haven't we had this before? It's so much better than the trout we catch," Charly says.

"And there are no bones. It's boneless," Adrian says.

The napkins usually covered in the thin trout bones are smeared with light pink.

"But you didn't," I say.

"What?" Charly asks without looking up from his food.

"Catch it," I say.

After dinner I clean up and retreat to bed. Everett has not broken any of the contract, but something about him bringing the salmon keeps me awake. When my brother and I were children, we fished with our father most weekends during the season. My brother refused to clean the fish, claiming the smell of their slit open bodies churned his stomach. One afternoon we'd fished to our limit, and he placed each fish onto newsprint covered picnic table. I cut the fish from anus to gill, ripped the organs from their bodies. I had just celebrated my eighth birthday, and was proud of this skill, something my father awarded with a rare compliment. When I opened one of the smaller fish, hundreds of tiny pink eggs spilled out onto the newsprint. It wasn't the first time this had happened, but my brother had turned away and vomited into the bushes. My father had teased my brother's weak stomach, and tasked him with dumping the gut-bucket into the lake.

The next morning I call Everett and ask for him to come over, claiming I need some advice, some expertise in dealing with the boys' choices. In truth, I haven't opened the yellow envelope yet. I hate the idea I've lured my boys into some sort of subconscious confession, but I can't risk letting them become what their blood tells them to be. When I first found out I was pregnant, I prayed for a girl—you have some say in protecting a victim, but a person compelled by something as powerful as hunger is much harder to control. I knew when I chose the photos for Everett to present to them, two of women in their twenties, two of women in their mid-teens, and one, only one, of a six-year-old girl, I was asking for information that might force me into drastic actions.

"Of course, ma'am. I'd be happy to." There is a catch in his voice and he clears his throat and I realize I haven't alleviated yet.

It hadn't even occurred to me minutes after I rolled over to shut off the alarm, or even when I pressed my skin into the hot stream of the shower. I can't remember the last time it hasn't been the first thing I thought of upon waking.

The boys prepare to go fishing, as they do every Friday in the summer. They exchange comments about the bone-ridden bodies of trout, its meat so minimal you have to eat an entire family to feel full. I pack lunches: egg salad sandwiches and apples, beef jerky to pass the time on the bank waiting for the fish. They will walk the mile to the river, sit on the lawn chairs they leave there all summer, and stay until they have enough for dinner and the day after lunch. Without distractions, my boys have very practical and useful skills. They don't yet know how most their age choose to use their bodies.

Everett arrives two hours after the call while I'm scrubbing egg and bacon from the breakfast frying pan. I feel the vibration of his knock on the screen door on parts of my body that haven't been touched since the boys' father left nine years ago.

"Come on in." I rinse the pan with the spray gun, bubbles raise, riot, then disintegrate.

"Thank you so much for coming." He doesn't get a chance to speak before I'm on my knees and unzipping his jeans. He flinches when I scrape his skin with my teeth, and I press his hips against the counter. His palms hover on either side of my head, their heat pinks my ears. I stand and push him toward the stairs. He moves too slowly so I grab his wrist until he follows me upstairs like a child dragged to his room.

He yanks his hand away at my doorway, but his penis is erect and protruding from his jeans.

"Get on the bed," I say.

"I don't think this is a good idea." He says this like a question.

"Get on the bed," my voice quieter and steadier for the repetition.

There is part of me that wants him to rip me apart, literally, finish me before I do what I must do. But he resists only verbally: "we shouldn't," but unbuckles his pants and lies on the bed.

In the split second before I'd kneeled in front of him I thought instead of smashing the frying pan against his head— one blow to knock him down then fifty more until his face and skull and brains were no longer distinguishable from one another. The yellow envelope was open on the kitchen table, and he'd only glanced at it before my mouth was on him. Post-it notes indicated Adrian's choice: one of the women in her twenties, and Charly's: the six-year-old.

When I finish with Everett, I rest my chest on his. The room is thick with the smell of our bodies: musky, thick, tinny. Bodily fluids streak the sheets in inarticulate patterns. Aside from the steady rhythm of his breath, he is still. For the first time since the boys' father left, sickened by the history he'd begged me to share, I am fully alleviated. My body no longer a distraction, I get out of bed, lock the bedroom door with Everett asleep inside, and descend the stairs.

One night my mother opened my door just as my brother, naked from the waist down, had pulled back my covers. I sealed my eyes on hers, willing her to finally understand, to yank him away and beat or suffocate him until his body lay as still as meat. She'd called his name, then said, "Poor boy, sleepwalking again," and led him from my room. I don't believe my mother loved him more than me, or that she didn't want to protect me, but rather than she'd already failed in doing so, so she focused on protecting the other.

Downstairs I prepare: Charly must be taken care of while I'm still alleviated. The pills crumble under the pressure of the spoon. The boys will soon return with their bounty, fish slit, cleaned, strung through the mouth on a bobbing line. They will measure the length of each fish and debate the better fisherman. They will laugh and joke as though it doesn't really matter as long as there is enough to eat and Charly will be dead before the hiss and splatter of dinner cooking has stilled.

Runaway Boy

Once, there was a boy that walked into a river. There was a particular point of access the boy knew well. He and his brother once lay on the river bank, tied hooks to fishing line and fished for bullheads. He remembered the spike and stupid faces in the split second before they burst between the rock and their sneakers. The fish had been so easy to catch here—too easy—the thrill of the wet crunch long gone by the time they stopped stomping.

The mud of the bank cooled and cracked under his belly from the memory, so he lay in the warmth of the same spot. He noticed the pyrite glint from the other side of the river. There was something there to remember, but he resisted, moved his nose close to the mud and inhaled the wormbox scent. Back when there *was* fishing, his mother would fill a wooden box with worms coaxed from the dampened lawn. Every morning she lifted back the massive lid with splintered fingers while the he and his brother dumped egg shells and orange peels and carrot tops for the worms to laboriously translate into fertilizer for the spring garden.

He dipped his orange-dust fingertips into the water. He couldn't see the bottom though he knew it was only a foot or so deep. When he stepped in, its bed received his foot before he noticed the chill. Once, when he'd stepped wrong and a nail slid into the sole of his barefoot, his mother said the foot was as important as a brain, tasked with understanding the earth it walked on before it took a step. He burrowed it in the mud, trying to learn the language of the river bed and brought in the other once it made sense.

As his body lay flat on the river's surface, he realized he'd never really felt temperature the way others seemed to. He understood, rather than felt, that the river would drain the warmth from his body the way he knew to skirt the campfire, flinch away from flame, test with the tongue before taking a bite.

Resting on the skin of the river, he noticed the trees. They were tall and green and absorbed the wind with their ribs. Mountains thrust skyward and stitched the sky ragged. Below him, the fish with heads nothing like bulls divided the water with their bodies. He thought about his brother, who at first resisted the killing. Was his brother still everywhere else but here? As the surface of the river relented, he focused on what he remembered of his brother. He conjured his scent— the smear of his sweat on his own skin when they wrestled; the sweet-sour of bubble gum on his breath; even the foul air of his waste when he refused to flush. And those he never got to smell on him—the peppery musk of aftershave, the yeasty tang of beer, the blood of a first fight.

The water hushed into his ear canals, and then his eyes were under. The surfaced world gave up its reliance on borders and edges: branches became beaks, summit became sun. *Shhh*. Not silence, but *Shhh*. He wondered if the sky ever got tired of above, of giving back. Baseballs. Kites. Prayers. Tiny astronauts from Fourth of July Rockets. Brothers.

Here, the river said as it pulled back its blanket of mud, *Rest here*.

The boy, too tired for more wondering, rested.

Who can know what it took to be saved? Who knew who wanted to be saved when it came to the point of last chance? The child felt a prick on his side, which became a tug, then a tear. The river gave back, too. Branches again were branches, and the sun, now without a summit, a sun. He saw something familiar on the mountainside. Shadows, angles, the bristle of a tree line. You could find a face anywhere if you knew how to look.

II.

The boy knew nothing about climbing a mountain, but he put on his tennis shoes, packed a ham and cheese sandwich, soda, and a compass in a knapsack and set out for the climb. The base of the mountain was surrounded by evergreen, fern, and fallen logs soft with termites. The boy and his brother had camped near here with a neighbor and his son only months before.

Their mother had been hesitant about the neighbor's offer to take the brothers along, but the guilt about activities she believed belonged to father and son (camping, fishing, killing things and making them meals) had worn her down. The neighbor had whittled sticks for roasting while the boys gathered twigs and moss for the fire. The boy knew it had happened, the camping trip, but could only remember it as something he'd heard about second hand. He guessed his brother had wormed his sleeping bag close to his own when the night, the real dark of it, opaqued the space between hand and face. It could've happened differently, of course.

When the boy stopped for his lunch, he saw the skin of his hands were rough and porous as granite. Time had passed, but he couldn't say how much, but he could see a different country, the country where he was born but not his brother or mother. His mother had claimed it a good thing—the differences in their birth country, how that made them unique. But he'd never wanted to be unique. He wanted to belong to what his brother belonged to, to always be in the place he was.

On the camping trip, the neighbor had told them about the various local species one could eat if necessary. He'd stamped his boot on a rotten log and revealed its bounty: beetle larvae, termites, the deep purple of a moth pupa. The neighbor had eaten a grub, and the boys groaned when they'd heard its skin pop. The neighbor had laughed then stopped laughing. *You never know what you'll have to do to survive.*

The boy retrieved his sandwich, fumbled with twist tie on the baggie. His fingers refused to bend, as did his knees and elbows. He imagined an ache in his joints but didn't feel one. He managed to pop open the soda, but his throat resisted the swallow. He lay on the ground and pressed between the atmosphere and the resistance the earth offered. There was warmth and the quiet throb of the world when nobody was noticing. Squirrels must've chattered, birds must've called things as they saw them. Wind must've stiffened the thousands of tiny hairs on his body when it lifted, then settled, the scent from a dead thing. His sight must've been the last to go—its slow fixation on the massive stretch of sky. Could it be this easy?

They'd never again camped with the neighbor, but they set up end-of-it-all scenarios to practice what he'd taught them. They ate like they'd had nothing to, then twisted dried moss and held it to flint. And when the freeze hit, and it was the last sleeping bag on earth, they slid in, spoon-like, and did what they had to keep warm.

A thousand seconds or days or years could've passed. Mountains pay no attention to the passage of time. But then an awareness, more pressure than pain, like a cat on the chest. Soon, sight: a face instead of sky, mouth instead of motion. His name on the wind instead of the stench. Then the scent—the first one he'd seared into memory, a smell only he and his brother could claim their own. And then, the pain only being born can cause. Stone to skin hurt much more skin to stone.

III.

The boy entered an overgrown garden. There were many herbs he recognized, and he pinched parsley from its stem, let it burst on his tongue, wedged it between his teeth like a joke. He found chocolate mint, and its bitter reminded him of Sunday afternoon ice cream cones. He loved chocolate chip mint, which was also his mother's favorite.

His brother's favorite was bubble gum—he'd suck away the ice cream, save the gum for later. Sometimes, his brother shared the gum with him. They agreed how gross it was—this kind of exchange, then blew bubbles bigger than each other's. When the boy couldn't see the garden's entrance, he sat in the dirt. It always came to this, he thought, the sky above and earth below. He put the gun in his mouth and pulled the trigger. The worst wasn't the bullet. Or the bloat. Or the burst. Or the rot. It was the bloom.

In the cool, dank dirt of January, he bred without discretion. He split himself underground, rearranged the dirt with growth's insistence. Now, instead of a single suffering, he suffered by the dozens. His blossom was mostly purple, but white scattered the patch like an accident. He'd never feared bees, never been stung, but when the queen honeybee, nearly starved from the bloomless winter, landed in his bowl and dusted itself heavy with pollen, sometimes even wedging in for the night when the sun set, it was excruciating.

The boy felt nothing of the early spring bloom delight. He stood a little taller each morning, unfurled when the sun demanded it, and collapsed inward when it let him go. At dawn one day, when he loosened his grip and the tight pull of petals relented, he sensed a familiar presence. He leaned into it, inhaled so its scent had no choice but to become his breath. He tucked it root-deep, where it couldn't just be gone from one day, at least not without taking him with it.

By the time he heard the thwack of the hoe, a hundred brothers surrounded him, each an imprint of itself, of himself, and this mattered, but not more so than the presence of their mother, whose tool cleaved the earth as she ripped him from its throat. In the clutch of his mother, his roots dangled like veins. His brothers, roots still part of the earth's tangle, carried on. What the earth offered, it also took back.

IV.

The boy was born of air. The wings were a surprise, though not unwelcome, as he'd always been sky-bound. From the sky, the desperation of land to be anything other than itself was clear. Once, he and his brother had spun themselves sick and collapsed onto the ground, faces skyward, the prick of a thousand blades of grass only a tickle on the blemish-free skin of their backs. The sky wasn't birdless that day, but it was in that moment, and the clouds became anything they needed them to be: a wispy flay of a horse's tail, a bullseye, destroyed landscapes of imagined tragedies.

They told each other elaborate stories with heroes and villains, battle and retreat, promise of happiness or horror, until the clouds moved on and they were left with nothing but the blue. His mother was everywhere in that blue, thrusting trees upward, each offering the sweet relief of rest if he would just land, come back to where he'd come from. He saw the angles of his mother's face in the apex of the branches, her hair in its splattering of needles. Nests, in all likeliness, or nipples if you needed to feed.

He flew on. The muscles strapped to his wings tore, but he willed them down, then up, and when they were more meat than muscle, he let the wind do the work. Maybe it would be different this time, he thought, as skin forced the feathers from his body. Maybe this time there wouldn't be a brother, and whatever suffering would be his own. Could it be that suffering is all he wanted? His talons retreated and toes appeared. His black hole eyes reclaimed their areole of blue. He landed in the arms of his mother, naked as a newborn, and she brought his mouth, now unobstructed by beak, to her breast and said, *Eat.*

V.

The inconsistent motion of the sea was a relief. No sky to pin him down, no soil to surface him. His bough read the sea as if he were sighted, noticed where it lulled when he should've been thinking of its lift. Transformation wore on him, but he flared his sails like the broad chest of a man. The winds pressed him here and there, reached underneath, around, inside, and he let them.

The memories of his brother were now his own. If he could reach, his fingers would find thick hair where things were once smooth. He would find his body responded to others as it once only responded to itself. If he'd had an older brother he might ask him about it. It didn't care about motive: it didn't care about who, when, or why.

A storm swelled the sea's skin, grayed its bright blue like a bruise beyond the point of explanation. His bough sulked, each surfacing like a new tragedy. He thought of the sea creatures that evolved with each new disaster, never wondering *What for?* His sails, frayed by the teeth of the wind, lost their hunger for resistance. Is it finished yet, he wondered. It must be almost finished. Why did things so often refuse to end? He knew his mother would never give up. She'd promised, *If you run away, I will run after you.* Why couldn't she just crack his burden boards and sink him? And now she was the wind? What did he do to deserve such love?

He was shored without answers. His body was body, not boat or bough. This time he was a grown man. The air was still, so when he stood his skin didn't bump from its chill. His penis was much longer than he'd imagined it would ever be, and his testicles throbbed. He looked for something to cover up with (his mother could've been anywhere) but there was only sand and sea and sky. The ache erupted into his gut and he felt pressure in the bulb of his eyes. He vomited saltwater and seaweed, then chunks of himself that looked like raw steak. The heat of sun on skin was unbearable. He palmed his penis—relief was quick and terrible. His body shivered in the cool hush of the breeze.

VI.

The boy, made a man too soon, was the main attraction. The circus has never been short on trapeze artists, but one with the unique physical condition such as his was an instant hit. His mind was that of a child's, but his body was in high demand. They slipped into his tent after the show, when he was weak from carving the air sixty feet high. He couldn't claim he didn't like the surge of storm in his stomach as he chalked his hands, gripped the bar, and soared. He hoped to someday let go. In his bed, he didn't pay much attention to the breast cupped in his hand or nipple that his tongue drew taut. The men gasped at the sight of him, held their own penises in their palms like money. He learned it was faster to use his mouth than his hands, so he did. It wasn't always as bad as it sometimes could be.

He didn't wonder what his mother would think of what he was doing. Some days he was confused by his memories—they must belong to him, but they didn't gut him like they would someone who lived them. He watched a face so much like his own cracked open in pain. He saw a body (his?) bent, folded, become a thing meant only for the want of another. In this memory, the rungs of the ladder bisected his soles as he climbed toward the power lines. The deepest part of his ear vibrated with lines' hum. From here, he saw another country, but didn't know why it was something worth seeing. He saw the bay where one winter he waded in waist deep on a dare. He saw his legs push forward, and the tendrils of seaweed trying to tangle him still. A series of grunts shattered the vibration, a warm wet leaked from his body. He jumped from the ladder, and before he could think *let go*, his hands gripped the trapeze bar and swung him back to the circus tent.

From the tight rope, a woman, unwisely, used his body as a focal point. She was dressed like a little one, pink tutu, lace and sequence, ruffles and camisole. Her feet molded around the tight rope like clay. Even from the distance, he recognized her cotton candy eyes, the tips of her ears, more point than curve, her nose that twitched with the scent of him. The trapeze swung him back and he saw the scene like he'd never before. A clown galloped around the arena, neighed and whinnied to make the crowd laugh. A donkey walked on its back hooves, peeled back its thick black lips to smile at the applause. He looked at his body and saw the shape of his engorged penis under his leotard. Like everyone else he wondered what he would do differently if given the chance.

VII.

His mother opened the front door before his footsteps on the stairs announced his presence. His lips were so dry, and when he licked them he tasted the dust from the chips he only got to have when camping. Body only a boy's, raspberry scabs on his knees, shoes untied. She took him into her arms and he rested his cheek on her shoulder. He was cold, so she lit a fire and brought flannel pajamas. She held one pant leg open then the other and he slipped into them and hopped onto her lap. They read books without words so they could make their own stories and decide exactly what happened. They took turns, each always showing up in the other's version. They held each other's gaze, blinked only when their eyes insisted. When he said he was hungry, his mother brought a bowl of the orange-dust chips, didn't even make him share.

Outside, a scarecrow warned the crows to find another. Tomatoes, finally free of the sun's bullying, stretched their bodies bright. The sky was still the sky, the asterisks in it just stars, and the moon was made exactly of what it was made of.

The Intakes

Mary wasn't the sort of person that saw one thing and thought it another, so when her gaze was snagged away from feeding the hoof-troughed and chuffing pigs and toward the fence at the back of their property, she knew what she was looking at was a woman, barely thicker than the fence post she hid behind, her hair a riot of red. Strangers weren't unheard of in their neighborhood, but she'd been warned about those that slinked around instead of parking in the driveway and knocking on the door. She'd heard of spottings like this—gaunt women with skin like beef jerky watching from the edges. Or fat with not-good-enough, leaving messages, sloppy with bawl, on answering machines. She met these stories with a *Poor Thing*, like one might squirrel that didn't think to look both ways.

She lifted the grain bucket and walked through the mud to the barn. The cows twitched their ears at the bucket's eek and the thunk of its rim against the feeding platform. They filed through the barn's door and swished the grain into their mouths with foot long tongues. She thought she should mention the sighting to Oliver, and probably to Grace, but it could wait. Her pockets were still full of seeds and the chickens were waiting for the scatter.

As the chickens stabbed at the food and each other, she looked to the property's edge. The woman was still there, though now was kneeling, hands parting the tall grass like curtains. She wore sunglasses with lenses the size of tea saucers. The sun was positioned so that the lenses flared on her face like twin stars. It figures, she thought, such a woman would wear sunglasses instead of a hat. Bellies full, the cows pocked the field, chewing, digesting, surging their tongues brain-toward, tails stilling flies with their snap.

In the kitchen, Oliver cracked eggs into a pan slick with bacon grease. This wasn't an every day—their bodies were taut with the knowledge of moderation. Mary brought her fingertips to Oliver's shoulders, worked them deep into the muscle. The day before he'd rototilled the garden, raked it level, dragged the three-pronged row-maker until there were ninety-nine. His muscles refused to belly up for her fingers, so she sat at the table and drank the coffee he poured.

Oliver clanked a plate with eggs, flecked green with spinach and cilantro, in front of her. Something in the kitchen hummed with electricity, clicked, hummed a lower octave. Their forks scraped and mugs clunked while they ate without speaking. An intake was scheduled for today, and once the infant arrived the racket would considerable. Oliver seemed less bothered by the disruption than Mary—sometimes it seemed he even enjoyed what they demanded of him: washed shit and spit up away without grimace, lay their bodies, limbs frantic with too much room to move, in their crib and closed the door.

Before their first intake, Grace had told Mary she might have a physical reaction to the infant's screams, and to not be surprised if she noticed tiny pinpricks around her nipples, or a tightening of muscles in her lower abdomen, even though what would cause such a throb was years gone, but she hadn't noticed anything like that. Instead she felt a pressure at the base of her skull, and a throb in the pit of her ears, far out of reach of a cough or Q-tip.

After breakfast, Mary went to the barn for the wheelbarrow. When she slid back the heavy wood door, she heard a gasp, then the tap-tap of tip-toe. The barn smelled like a scrape unbandaged too soon. The pig was only days dead, and even with all the precautions, the butchering of an animal always left a scent that took weeks to dissipate. Mary knew the woman watched her from the loft, even knew which bale of hay she was hiding behind. Grace had once instructed her to avoid eye contact and conversation if such a meeting were to occur, so she lifted the hoe from the rack of gardening tools, clunked it in the wheelbarrow. When she dragged the door closed it sounded like thunder.

Oliver kneeled at the garden's edge, wrote *Peas, Corn, Carrots, Broccoli, Kohl Rabbi, Radishes* onto pieces of kindling to mark the rows. Even the most dissimilar vegetables were difficult to distinguish from one another when they first pierced the soil. She stepped into the prints his boots had left from the previous day's leveling and scooped up the earth until identical holes spotted the rows. She knew she should tell Oliver about the woman in the barn, but the work of the garden demanded the quiet. She dropped five peas into each hole, replaced the dirt she'd scooped aside. They existed like this for some time: her navigating the garden in tracks he left; him figuring the layout in a notebook and labeling the kindling; the woman locked in the barn, eyes squinting through the loft window.

The intake was supposed to come after lunch, and when Oliver said it was time to go in, they hadn't finished the planting. This bothered Mary, this prioritizing, this rationality, so when he pulled back the shower curtain to invite her in, she stepped in but made him get out, though his body was still slick with soap. She showered quickly without soap or even wetting her hair. When she entered their bedroom, he was tightening his belt. She undid it, dragged down his pants so quick her fingernails left thin red tracks. *We don't have time for this*, she figured he was thinking, but he knows better than to complain. She lay on the bed, grasped his head until he lowered his face between her legs.

Mary thought about the woman in the loft, wondered if she has found a way out. Once she'd found a batch of kittens tucked into a cavern between the hay bales. Their mews so thin the air broke them. They were pre-sight, ears pinned to their heads. She'd lifted each, held their shrimp-shaped bodies to her neck, the part of her she thought most like the belly of their mother. When she told Oliver what she'd found, he'd said, *You shouldn't have touched them.* She'd accused him of being heartless, but knew he was the opposite. He said nothing when she came to him after surprising the mother cat the next day, who'd already eaten three kittens, and was halfway through a fourth.

She came quickly, made more a scene of it than necessary, and he kissed her on the mouth and left the room. She watched the window for any sign of the woman, a flutter of her spaghetti hair, blink of her cow-like brown eyes. Only minutes later Grace's car pulled into their driveway and she heard the muffled, even sound of greeting someone you've always known.

When Mary joined them in the living room. Oliver lifted the infant and said, *It's a boy.* The skin at the corners of his eyes curved from his smile. He walked past her and the darkened hallway to the infant's room swallowed them both.

Grace approached her, lifted the diaper bag from her shoulder and looped it over Mary's.

Same as last time, she said. *Just one week here and we'll place him.*

The diaper bag tag read, *This Bag Belongs to David,* but they weren't supposed to use his name. Mary ruffled through the bag as though there might be something in it she wanted. It was packed with diapers and pajamas. They used to bring blankets to swaddle the infants, but found it slowed the process.

Grace patted her shoulder on her way out. Mary said goodbye, but not until Grace was already out the door. From the porch she watched Grace get into her car, rotate her neck to the road to check for cars, and ease out onto it. The porch smelled like dead flies, and she made a note to vacuum the window sills.

She felt Oliver's hands on her shoulders before she heard him.

We can finish now, he said, and she thought he meant the sex until he nodded toward the garden. The infant tantrumed in the bedroom. She followed Oliver outside. The intake made Oliver chatty, but she didn't bother with the meaning of his words. She had been surprised when Grace had called early that morning. Oliver's face had been smeared with loss when Grace had come to pick up the last infant. He'd even tried to convince her the infant wasn't ready, that he needed a couple more days to make sure even though they all knew the infant would be dead in less than twenty-four hours if it stayed.

It was hours later when Mary returned to the barn with the gardening tools. When she pulled back the door, hot air, thick with dust, sent her into a fit of sneezing. The woman was a foot in front of Mary when she recovered. Up close, she could see that she was neither thin nor fat, but somewhere in between that would probably not be of note if you weren't thinking about it. Her scent mixed with that of the butchered pig's and reminded Mary of an ear infection. The woman had whipped her hair into one of those buns that used its own hair to stay put. Her mouth was open, top teeth halved by her upper lip.

Mary stepped back. Grace had warned them about the women that get this far, how their desperation smelled like milk on the edge of curdle, and that they were capable of anything. More often than not, they just wept, begged, offered money, or themselves, screamed *You have no idea, You have no right, How would you feel if,* but sometimes they carried knives or guns, stabbed or pointed them into the air, dared people to make them use them. One woman had even set herself and the infant on fire in the intake couple's living room. The couple survived, but the infant died, as did the woman, of course. So often people suffering forgot to think things through.

The woman lay on the barn's cement floor before Mary noticed the shovel in her hands. She'd killed living beings before—shot the pig, hacked off the heads of chickens, twisted the neck of that mother cat— it wasn't as hard as one might think. She put the cutting edge to the woman's throat, brought her foot the shovel's shoulder. The woman looked younger from here, Mary thought, and she noticed an earring in the shape of a hummingbird and a tattoo of a wing just below her earlobe. A sales tag from was tucked into the back of her shirt. The buttons were one off. Mary grabbed a rag from the shelf and pressed it to the woman's cut. When Mary lifted her so she and the woman were elbow to armpit, the bun failed and her hair spilled like hay. The woman groaned, but her body refused the resist. Mary pulled her up the stairs to the loft, the woman's head resting in the cave of her chest.

It had never been easy for Mary to feel anything but just fine. She didn't believe things meant something other than what they did. Seeds split with stem and stem split soil because that's what they were meant to do. Animals happily greeted her every morning because they were eager for the meal. Oliver lifted the blankets and drew her close because the body craved warmth. Things didn't cause her sadness, nor joy, which was a fact that evoked in her neither pain nor pleasure.

Mary lay the woman near the window. She dragged a bale close, slit the twine and loosed the hay. She covered the floor with a layer, dragged the woman onto it. She freed more and made a thicker layer for a pillow. More than likely the bleeding had stopped, but she left the rag alone. She looked out the window through the spot the woman had wiped clear earlier. The sky was more moon than sun, but neither put up much of a fight.

*

When Mary entered the kitchen, Oliver's hand was wrist deep in a chicken. He nodded toward two glasses of wine. She rarely drank, but something about its mercury glow made her crave the tangy bite. She took a drink, then held his glass to his lips. It dribbled down his chin, and she touched the tip of her tongue to each drop. One hand was still in the chicken, but he lifted her shirt with the other, brushed his thumb against her nipple. She pulled his head to her nipple. This was how they stayed: he didn't slip his fingers into her underwear. She didn't flatten her hand between his belt and skin. Mouth and nipple. Body and body. Giver and given.

The infant's cry burst the night. Oliver lifted his face to her level, kissed her, turned his attention back to the chicken. He told her to sit, relax, drink her wine. He put the chicken in the crockpot and went to the infant to change its diaper. She knew he would do so quickly with mouth and throat closed. Even a hum risked a moment of comfort for the infant, and that would only make things harder in the long run.

As a general rule, it took one day for an infant to feel hunger, seven to die from it. Nobody wanted the infants to die, of course, just to break them of the want of the mother. The point where the mother was no longer a part of the equation of life or death. Grace had told Mary she'd been one of the easiest infants to usher through the process, and that as a young child she'd only come to Grace when an injury was somewhere Mary couldn't herself address.

Oliver returned to the kitchen, poured himself another glass of wine and sat beside her. He coaxed one of her feet from where she'd wedged it into the couch's cushions. When she first moved in with him, he followed her around constantly, always wanting to touch her, not necessarily in a way that would lead to sex, just to have his body in contact with hers. They found her feet to be the middle ground. He moved his thumbs in a concentric motion on the ball, increasing the pressure until she coughed, lowered them to the arch. He watched only what he was doing, confident of how her body would respond. Within minutes, her nausea lifted, and he again lowered his thumbs to the part of the foot that, if such still belonged to her body, would've relieved the dull ache of menstrual cramps, coaxed the egg to the south of the body, relaxed the clench of the cervix during labor.

Oliver always took extra time with this part. She'd once asked him what the point was, but didn't complain when his fingers worked into the deep of the arch. She wondered about the way the body rearranged after what it clearly considered a trauma. Did the other organs stretch out, become less reliant on boundaries to tell them where they belonged? Oliver had never been anything but compliant in her decision to have the surgery, but she knew what he would've been if she'd chosen differently.

When the feeling became more obligatory than appreciated, she stuffed her foot back between the cushions. He left the room, and she heard the soft clink of the lid of the crock pot, and the hiss of spices being added. When he returned he had a blanket and pillow. The infant would need to be changed in the middle of the night, he told her, and he didn't want to disturb her sleep. Mary finished her wine and went to bed.

Mary woke from a dream about planting the garden. They planted according to Oliver's notes, marked carrots with the stick marked *Carrots* and so on, positioned the sprinkler so it watered the plants, not the grass or the field. Her wrist ached, probably from gardening, she thought, and at that moment she remembered dragging the woman up the stairs into the loft.

For the first time it occurred to her the woman might be hungry. Who knew how long it had taken for her to get to their property, or how well she'd taken care of herself up until that point. In the kitchen, the air was thick with the scent of rosemary and garlic and chicken. It had been eight hours, and the meat released the bone without hesitation. Mary put some on a plate, then sliced in apple in strips thin as paper. She wasn't sure whether or not the woman's jaw had been injured from the shovel.

It was rare she was outside in the middle of the night, so she took a minute to look up. The sky was flecked with stars. There was a brief time when constellations had interested her, but she eventually had given up on them. No matter how much she studied them, perusing sketches of how their coordinates translated into the chariot, the warrior and his shield, the beauty and her rock, she only saw points of light in a dark sky. Coyotes yipped in the field, some drawing the sound out until it was more haunt than howl.

The air in the barn had cooled into tolerable. Now that the sun wasn't forcing itself through the windows and onto the cement floor, she saw the stain from the pig slaughter. She balanced the plate of food on one palm and held the handrail of the stairs and climbed.

The woman was where she had left her. Mary positioned the woman upright against the wall and the window. She watched her chest for the rise and fall of breath. When she woke, Mary would tell her, even though it was against the rules, that they were only following the wishes of the infants. Couldn't she see they have a right to choose what they will love? What they can and cannot live without? She might not resist smacking her across the face to be taken seriously, then ask, *How selfish can you be,* she'd ask, *to want to cause your child the suffering of someday losing you?*

The woman's head slumped so that she appeared neckless. The light of the moon made the blood on her face look like chocolate. Her mouth hung open, so Mary slipped in a piece of shaved apple. She took the woman's hands, flipped them so the palms were skyward, and set the plate on them.

Eat if you're hungry. I'm not going to feed you, she said.

After she'd broken the mother cat's neck, the fourth kitten fell from its mouth. At that point, it was only belly, hind legs, tail. She'd brought the two living kittens into the house, lay them lined a box with a fleece blanket when she wasn't holding them or feeding them with a dropper. Oliver had retrieved the mother cat and the half-eaten kitten and buried them in a hole deep enough nothing would dig them up. The other two kittens didn't live long enough to open their eyes. Though they never spoke it, they both knew it was Mary's scent on the kittens that forced the mother to do the one thing she could to protect them.

The plate of food slid to the floor. Mary put the meat and apple back onto the plate—the last thing they needed was a loft full of rats. She pulled the woman's legs so her torso no longer rested against the wall. Without the moon to illuminate her face, she looked more like a shadow than a woman.

Mary heard Oliver calling to her from the house. She waited until it stopped, then descended the stairs and left the barn. She heard the infant's tantrum from its tucked away room, saw the light flood its window. She walked past the coop, where the chickens had stilled their throaty chuckling. Past the pen, where the pigs dreamt snout to snout, legs jerking with want of the trough. Past the cows that spotted the field like huge black boulders. She reached the barbed-wire fence that had been bent to fit a woman. A swatch of fabric dangled from one of the barbs. She worked it free and stuffed it into her pocket. The grass still was crushed into a woman-shape, so she got on her knees and looked back toward the house, and into the lighted window, where Oliver stood, infant in his arms, bodies like a dark constellation in a lit sky.

The Forgetting

She is at first the slick black of a seal in an already dark ocean. It is only four pm, but the sky is already more bruise than bright. The waves offer then take her back, each surge flashing an undeniable: the fish-belly white of arm; the sparkly fuchsia flush of dress up footwear. It is obvious and yet we still hope for the aquatic. We say to each other *You never know*, though we're mothers. We've never not known.

We see the men in the yellow jackets down shore and signal them as arranged. We leave untouched what we are desperate to press into our chests, which are stupid with heat and heartbeat, and let the shiver of her body chill us for good. We wait, shored. Seagulls keep their distance but chatter about who gets what first. Some keep their *Mine* deep in their throats, more a cackle than the bawdy giggle of others. The men, who've already forgotten the others they've recovered, rush toward us in a flurry as though the *RESCUE* on their jackets is what they do.

We are a mile inland when they pronounce her dead. There is nothing about what they say that hasn't already been forced from our mouths, and nothing they've seen will sour their dreams and wake them soaked with the sea of their bodies and skin flooded with the prick of panic. We find her mother at home, as advised. She stands in the kitchen mashing pears into sauce. She knows what we mean. We move quick because we are full of a throb that threatens to burst us. She doesn't fight us, but her feet jerk with some ancient last smudge of *Survive*.

*

The girl's name is Meredith Maris. Her mother's, Heather Hall. We add these details to the records of who is born and who dies. There is more to them than their names, and we add that information to the Book of Remembering. Heather loved hiking and reading books about birds and plants. She wished she'd married Meredith's father instead of the man she'd fallen in love with. Meredith loved catching common animals: snails, slugs, beetles, and seeing how long she could keep them alive. Heather was friendly but not kind. Meredith was mature but not wise. They were both loved and unloved, but that last part isn't transcribable so no one writes it down.

It's after midnight when we finish recording. Some of us go home to our children, living or not. Some stay in the center to read night into day. Some of us have people waiting up for us, or prepared to claim as much, to ask us what's wrong even though. We lift blankets and they settle like earth around us. Or grab a pillow and sleep on the couch. We climb onto the bodies beside us, wet ourselves with their mouths. Most of them have already forgotten why we were out. They don't ask *Where* or *Why*, or they do but forget their question before we bother to answer. These are the men whose hands we once slapped away from the lip of our underwear when all we wanted was to sleep. These are the men that once woke early enough to make us coffee and arrange fruit into smiley faces before leaving for work and returning in time to help with dinner. These are the men who, when cleaved with the tragedy of children they couldn't manage to keep safe, chose to forget, to stay tucked into the folds of the long term where they were the men we all thought they were strong enough to be.

When we've taken what we want from them, we swear to ourselves we've made the right choices about what to keep and what to release. To dip our feet into the suffering before stepping in, when to hold under and when to surface. We think about Meredith, wonder if the outfit she wore that morning was chosen as her last—what did she say to her mother when she last spoke to her? It is our job to suffer for her mother—it's the least we can do. It is messy. It tastes and smells bad. It hurts in a way that makes us say *Enough*. With this smeared all over our faces, we peer through the left-open bedroom doors of our children to suffer what we have or what we have lost.

*

When the first child went missing, we knew exactly what we needed to do. Organize. Search. Rescue. Recover. Grieve. Heal. We knew what to blame—the ocean and its insistence upon believing everything in its reach was its to take. Signs were posted: *Beware of Undertow; Sudden Drop Off: No Swimming Allowed.* After the third drowning, fences were installed and a lifeguard hired. A Coastline Watch was instated but they failed to see what they were there to not miss. Child after child found a way to let the ocean have its way and over and over we claimed we did everything we could.

Because it made sense to do so, there was an investigation into what the town had done to its children. What had been taken from them? What had been lost? What hadn't we seen though it was right in front of our faces? We looked at the schools. The drinking water. The community events where the majority of the town ate from the same batch of chili. We looked toward the sky. We looked at each other. We looked at ourselves. There was fault everywhere so everyone stopped looking.

*

The air is sour with blossom when Eddie Turntower's mother stands at the Town Council meeting and announces Eddie is haunting her. *Of course it must feel that way,* we say, and get back to the line item on the agenda: combining the elementary and secondary school. She slams her hands onto the desk. *Listen to me.* She says his bed is messy in the morning though she makes it every day. His hamper leans from the weight of his soiled clothing and we all know she's never slacked on laundry. She lifts a paper bag and shakes it toward the front of the room. Its crackle punctuates her words. From it, she pulls a t-shirt and pinches the shoulders in each palm and spreads it wide so we can see circles of sweat that darken the armpits and the splatter of a snack on its chest. She holds an armpit to her nose and breathes deeply. *Do you think I wouldn't recognize the smell of my own child's sweat?*

She passes the shirt to her right—each hand receives it reluctantly as an offering basket. When the shirt returns to her she folds it and puts it back into the bag. *There's more,* she says, and we listen to details about the crust of toothpaste in the sink, sneakers that refuse to stay branched on the shoe tree, the appearance of the feces he'd had a habit of forgetting to flush.

We stare at her. We listen. When she stops speaking we still stare. There's no reason to believe she isn't haunted. Why wouldn't she be, but what we aren't sure about is why that's a problem for her. Those of us who've lost would do anything for the slightest hint of our child. A quick sniff of hair dank with the sweat of fever. A misty shape just similar enough to be a *Could be.* A pressure at the back of our neck pulling us closer.

What do you want us to do? we ask after she walks out of the library. We look at one another because we know but can't say it.

The motion to merge the schools passes unanimously. What to do with the soon to be emptied building is tabled for next month. Pods of townspeople form outside the library. Men find themselves surrounded by one another. Women do the same. No one says a word about Heather and her ghost, but every voice is thick with them.

Our group forms that night. We make plans quick like we would during a disaster or a storm. Heather opens her front door. *We believe you,* we say, forcing the space between us visible with our breath. Inside she shows us all the places she's ghosted him. The air is foul. Piles of clothing scatter the living room floor. Bowls of unfinished cereal sit sogging on the counter.

Please excuse the mess, she says. *Growing boy…you know how it is?* She looks at us and we know this is our chance.

We understand. Take our hand, we say as we lead her to the bathtub. *He's waiting for you.*

Water won't be our way from now on—we don't want the ocean to think it's won—but this time it is. This time it has.

*

By mid-summer nine children are gone. One day Meredith becomes the tenth. Six mothers have been reunited with their gone. The rest are with us and we need them to help with the burden. Those that had fathers now have fathers that live in the bliss of the before. You'd have to ask them why. How. We can't be bothered with those questions when there is so much suffering to do. Our shoulders curl forward and down by the time each day is done though we know we only breathe right when they are up and back. When we walk, we are more horizontal than vertical, and the proof of what we've been up to as debatable as daylight.

Someday someone might look back and have ideas about how we could've handled this better and they will no doubt be right. We never claim to be without flaw—it's possible Heather could've healed, a few of us have, but how long can we stomach letting someone suffer when we have the answer to their relief?

*

Two weeks later a man in a skiff pulls Abigail Austen from a boulder fifty feet from the shore. Alive. It isn't clear if she'd changed her mind and swam to the rock or if the rock found her. We've learned some things we just don't get to know. The men respond to the fisherman's call but once it's clear she's alive they take her to the doctor and call us. Abigail's mother died when she was three and her father is a forgetter, so it's up to us. We are told when the fisherman found her she was bleeding from her hands and her face and her knee was bent the wrong way. The injuries on her hands and face are superficial, but the nurse lifts the gown to show us a six-inch bandage already rusted by the gash on her side.

Abigail is unconscious so we discuss options. We've never had a rescue. We aren't sure how to grieve for the survival of a child that found herself compelled to end her life but survived. We agree it's good her mother's dead. Our bodies buzz and we pick at our nails and scabs or sweep speckles of dandruff from our sweaters or bend over to retie shoes or tuck in things that are better left untucked. One of us throws up then more of us do. Machines beep and breathe as they were designed to do.

The doctor says it is uncertain she'll ever wake, so we decide to carry on as if she's lost. One of us knows Abigail love scones so we bake some and spread the butter on way to thick. Its salty smears glisten on our lips, our chins, the tips of our noses. The butter coats our throats so when we swallow nothing gets left behind.

Because she didn't have a mother, we don't know much about her so we make guesses. She loved to construct bird houses, certain if she got it right a mother bird would choose it to lay her eggs. She once took the top prize in children's Battleship Tournament. She and her best friend Meredith once build a raft out of branches and twine, wedging clay into the gaps between the branches. They were excellent swimmers, so no one stepped in when they launched it into lake, backs flattened against the branches, made bets about how long it would take until they sunk. Of course it never did.

The morning arrives without the skin of light. Our bodies are stiff and muscles on the cusp of seizing. The scones and their crumbs are gone and the butter worn from our throats by the insistence of swallow. Nurses ring our phones one at a time. Abigail is either dead or alive and nobody does anything to find out which.

There are no active *Missings*, but we decide to spend the morning on the beach. We used to spend mornings remembering how things once were: the shrieks and giggles of tide pool discoveries—sea cucumbers that eject then regenerate internal organs when threatened by predators; kites carving air into infinities before the nosedive; the opal backs of seals threading the skin of the ocean. It didn't take long for the burden of remembering so much for so many to ghost our own memories.

The tide is far enough out rocks we've never noticed constellate the shore. One of us points to the moon that hovers above the ocean, its shade a blister on the cusp of burst. Just beyond the *Warning* signs, dozens of jellyfish blob the beach, crimson hearts like open sores on the sand. Someone says certain jellyfish, when severely traumatized, can return to a polyp stage and start over. It is unclear, she says, if its memory starts over, too.

Down shore, the men in the yellow jackets watch us, or at least we think it is us they are watching. Their bodies move toward us, unburdened by grief, faces smeared with smiles. Have we got it all wrong? This insistence on remembering? What would we do if we had it to do again? It's becoming more difficult to remember who we once were or if we were ever once who we thought we were.

The men point at the jellyfish and shrug *Who knows* as they tiptoe through. Seagulls bitch and flap at them as if they know something we don't. By the time Eddie's body was found, the seagulls had eaten his eyes, nose, lips, earlobes and fingertips. Rendered senseless. We were told his mother refused to believe it was him even when they unzipped his sweatshirt and lifted his shirt to reveal a scar on his stomach from a childhood surgery. When the knowing took hold, they comforted by assuring her Eddie was certainly dead before the gulls got to him.

The men in the yellow jackets are closer than they've ever been. Once of them has covered himself in seaweed and stomps around moaning. The men laugh because they believe in make believe. Others balance rocks on other rocks, say *Oh, well* when they topple. Everywhere we look things are moving on.

If we were different women, we would leave the men to their play. We'd nod at the seagulls to let them know we understand why they do what they do, even though that is something we've never actually done ourselves: understand why we've done what we've done. We'd gather these transparent creatures in the bellies of our palms or the cradle of our arms and dive face first into the ocean. The men in the yellow jackets could save or sink us. Abigail could wake, mouth full of the why, or sleep and keep it secret. We'd let the ocean slowly coax us back, its waves like hands we craved on our bodies but never felt. We'd say *Remember.* We'd say *Forget.* We'd mean both.

What the Lonely Know

Elsa's knife has just cracked through the apple core when a smear of movement snares her gaze. Outside the window above the kitchen sink, a rope swing, still slick and tightly woven with lack of use ticks the tree with the knot before slitting the air with its tock. Wind that can whip a rope, flip a car, uproot an entire house from its foundation is something she's seen before, but the day is thick and still with the raunch of late summer. She quarters, then eighths the apple, carves the core away from each fraction's flesh, her movements quick hushes against pushy air. Something surges in her throat, then settles in her stomach. The lid to the peanut butter resists then offers itself to her palm with a soft pop—its salty-smooth calming the tang of the apple, and she forgets about the swing.

She sits at the table and gently slides the clumps of puzzle to make room for her plate. Once complete, twenty-two puppies of twenty-two breeds will have been reconstructed, but as of now, all that's apparent are a dozen or so bodiless faces. Her father had bought her the puzzle when she was eight and wanted a dog "more than life itself." Elsa had refused to open the box for months (why did people always think one thing could so easily replace another?), but one day she came down to find two plates full of strawberry waffles and her father separating the edges from the middles. Jordan, her husband, had recently rediscovered the puzzle, set it out to make the meals less tedious.

Elsa stares at the puzzle while scooping the portioned peanut butter onto each apple wedge. Something *eeks* the swing again, and her gut clenches. Somewhere someone mows the lawn. A plane drags itself across the skin of the sky, leaves a white scar. Sometimes she forgets where in time she is and for a split second thinks if she stepped outside, she might trip over her son's scooter and land in the world of two years ago. Or she might descend the porch stairs and smell the sweet hint of blossoms from the decade-dead apple trees. Maybe her father would be lying on cardboard under his turquoise pickup swearing about how tight the goddamned oil plug was. Maybe he'd be listening to the radio, and someone would be singing about a coat of many colors or what only the lonely know.

Elsa finds the mane-like fur of an Afghan and attaches it to the face it belongs to. Onto the poodle. These were the obvious ones she'd left for a day when she needed something to be easy. Eventually, a dozen years after her father had brought her the puzzle, she'd gotten the dog she always wanted, a Golden Retriever. It was a good dog. There was nothing particularly unpleasant about it. But she had yet to find getting something long wished for to be as good as the imagined.

When Jordan gets home from the park, his hair is smeared onto his forehead and the back of his neck in thick, dark strips. She can taste the sting of sweat before her lips touch his neck, smell the hint of curry from his lunch from across the kitchen. He clangs his keys on the counter and unhooks the leash from the dog's collar. The dog's tongue slaps water from its bowl like the water owes it an apology. She tosses the rest of the apple into the compost bin. Her stomach releases its grip and she takes a deep breath while it doesn't hurt. She knows she shouldn't, knows what it means that she wants it more with her blood than her body, but quickly her underwear are at her feet, skirt bunched around her hips. He's never found a reason to say no.

Afterward, she tells Jordan he can shower first. When she hears the screech of the curtain's hooks she wedges a pillow under her hips, focuses on contracting the muscles she once desperately tried to relax. It's when she finally relaxes that she thinks of what she saw by the swing. In this smudge of memory, she notices something blue behind the tall stalks of yellowed grass. Then something the shade of a crayon—red-orange, or orange-red. What she remembers is more color than shape and when she focuses, it dissipates like the flash of sun behind an eyelid. She stays horizontal, their fluids an expanding planet on the sheets beneath her hips. She doesn't mention it to Jordan when he spills from the bathroom in a fuss of steam. Whatever it was, it's hers. How it rolls and rests over the waves of consciousness. How it settles on her tongue, still as stone.

While he dresses, Jordan talks about what he's planned for dinner then about another dog at the park that theirs had taken a liking to. He says he exchanged numbers with its owner, since the dogs had gotten along so well, and maybe they'd all meet up one day and see how it went.

After a meal of lasagna, garlic bread, and Caesar salad, Jordan suggests a walk. Two years ago, she'd been more bone than body. The corner of her jaw, bulb of cheekbone, the curve of rib subtle as a tsunami under her skin. As a teenager she'd read that when the body is hungry enough it will feed on its own muscle—especially the heart. The information was meant to scare her and the girls in her Women's Health class, not into chubbiness, of course, but enough to make it sound like a state of being one should avoid. But it had fascinated her: she imagined the slow collapse of valves, the tedious digestion of atria and ventricle. The stubborn resilience of a body that would kill itself to stay alive.

The sky is the color of grapefruit until it meets the eggplant horizon. Jordan unleashes the dog and it bolts. They both know it will return with an offering: a rabbit or mouse with a snapped neck, and look to them for praise before slinking away in shame. The first time she'd found its offering, she'd held it by its cord-like tail in front of the dog's face and spoke a resounding *No*. Dogs are quick to accept blame, but it'd felt odd to punish it for doing what was made to do.

They walk the trail that outlines the perimeter of their property. Jordan grabs her arm when she takes a step that jars her hip. Her muscles contract against the semen that surges onto her underwear. Every day she finds new reasons to give up. It's much more land than they need, but her father had written into the will his wishes for her to keep it all. He'd been clear about how he'd wanted her life to be after he was gone, made elaborate plans to keep her from increased suffering.

Once on such a walk with her father, they'd seen a pack of coyotes—two adults and six pups edging the field. She'd never been so close, and her father lifted her onto his shoulders. The adult animals held their snouts low to the bodies of the pups, each howling more from the gut than the throat. The sound pressed into her ears like water, settled in the unreachable regions. They watched and listened until the coyotes quieted and retreated into the scattered ribs of the woods. It was then they'd seen that each pup had an angry mouth of cranberry flesh where a tail should've been. Her face pinked and fluid graveled her throat. Her father lowered her from his shoulders, told her to run ahead home before she could ask why.

The dog slinks under an old barbed wire fence that once kept their bull away from the cows. It enters the small shed that where they had often been stanchioned.

I'll get the dog, Jordan says.

I'll come, too.

You don't have to.

I know, she says, and steps on the bottom wire and lifts the middle. Jordan bends his body in half and lunges a leg through. Rabbits and mice could be excused, but the dog had once found a batch of kittens they knew had been born in the shed, and their bodies had ended up on their front step, wet, slick, and still as organs.

Jordan corners the dog in the shed and attaches its leash. Though it's been years since the bull had been there, she smells its thick, musky scent when she steps inside. She sees a scrap of bright red fabric caught on the splintered beams of the stanchion from where the bull often tried to tug its head free. She reaches for it, but it disintegrates between her fingers. Each spring for years the bull had awoken her with its early morning bellowing. The noise started deep and thick with throat before tightening into a screech. Her father warned her to stay the hell away from it, especially when the cows were in heat.

One Fourth of July, the bull had barreled through the fence, twenty-five feet of barbed wire in a flurry behind it. Within minutes, her father shot and killed it. Even though its meat would be tough, it could feed a family for a year, but its body lay in the yard rotting for hours. The next morning, though the bull no longer stuffed it full of its hollering, the cows stood in a line where the fence protecting their yard had been, their slobbery lowing clouding the air. She'd been in the yard since the sun had come up. Or maybe since the night before. Starlings scattered their songs from the crotches of trees. The moon sagged in the sky, a fading stamp of itself. She waited for something to end it—maybe the Russians would finally make good and she could step toward the flash and become shadow. Maybe the tectonic plates would finally force the fissure and let ocean reclaims its dryland. Maybe the Earth would unhook itself from the sun's bullying and give into the universe's, *Come here.*

But nothing ended. She'd have to suffer it. She'd continued to lay on a patch of grass already flattened into a shape like hers but smaller, unable to look away from the black hole eyes of a creature that was even more dangerous than anyone had imagined.

The dog fits into a tantrum of barking and she realizes she's on the shed's cement floor. Jordan's palms her armpits and helps her stand, his arms halo her until she steadies. Tight bright floaters burst then disperse in her periphery.

I don't know why that happened, Elsa says.

Let's go back, he says.

Let's go back, she repeats.

The dog bolts toward a shiver of motion in the field and Jordan lets go and the leash drags behind in a blue blur.

In the middle of the night she wakes from a dream about fireworks. In the dream, she holds lit ones, their fuses hissing sparks, the ones you're supposed to light on the ground and run. She keeps throwing them down, but others keep appearing in her palm, their sparks scatter her hand with red dot mouths of burned flesh. When she wakes, she scoots her hips back until they're cradled in Jordan's.

*

The next morning at breakfast Jordan reminds her it is Good Grief Group day. The kitchen has already been cleaned of his usual breakfast-making mess. A mound of scones cools on the counter. He's cooked bacon and already sliced and buttered her blueberry scone. She licks a mound of butter and swallows it to ease the path of the scone. Her therapists would argue otherwise, but she'd never worried the shape or size of her body. When she was finally able to gain weight, she was expected to discuss her feelings about it. Occasionally, the muscles of her lower back would seize and cause her a great amount of pain. The skin on her knuckles and elbows was wrinkled well beyond her age. Somedays she woke with a headache coffee wouldn't calm. She'd offer these statements in response to the questions of how she felt about the changes in her body—they were really the only complaints she had.

Okay, she said. So much of their lives consisted of him caring for her. That's something she'd like to talk about with the therapist. Not what's she's gaining. Not what she's lost. Jordan knows better than to watch her eat, so he lets the dog out and drags the vacuum into the living room where the group will gather. She eats while he vacuums, its hum occasionally catching and coughing when it finds something too hard to swallow.

After she finishes the scone and three pieces of bacon she watches the dog in the yard from the window above the kitchen sink. It finds a pile of shit Jordan missed, eats it, then bolts toward a squirrel skittering up the cherry tree where the swing hangs. When her father brought the swing home she'd watched him fussing through the complicated business of safety testing. He burdened it with his weight in various positions, swung himself vigorously to test its range of motion in relation to the tree's trunk. It was still a couple days before the Fourth of July but he'd been wearing his red, white, and blue baseball hat for days. Each time the aggressive swinging knocked it off he repositioned the hat and started again. He never spoke about patriotism or national pride, though he occasionally muttered curses about Ronald Reagan, but every year he'd dig the hat out from the winter gear bin. When he'd finally exhausted his list of possible disasters related to the swing, he stepped aside so it could be used as it was meant to be.

The dog tires of the squirrel and drops its nose to the grass to look for another pile. When Jordan had mentioned the dog's eating habits to the vet he'd assured him it was normal, a natural survival instinct, and that all we could do was keep the mess cleaned up.

The coffee pot hisses and gurgles. Jordan says the group will be there in twenty minutes and holds out the last piece of bacon to her. She eats it on her way upstairs. Though she rarely dresses with anyone else in mind it's only the third time she's met with these women and it matters to her that they think she looks like a woman who matters. She chooses black tights and a striped dress with a tiny pearl button that rests near the top of her vertebrae. She passes over the strappy red shoes and buckles black Danskos.

The women arrive in pairs or trios. Elsa watches them lumber up the driveway, cautious as school bus drivers, and park with plenty of space between each car. Their cars are silver or black or that non-committal shade a salesman might call champagne. The dog is too distracted with surviving in the backyard to bother barking. From their bedroom she hears Jordan greet each woman with the same tone—almost one of surprise, and thanks them for making the drive. When she enters the living room, he's already served coffee and set out the scones, butter, and is asking about cream and sugar.

Each woman, even the heavier ones, wears their damage like a skin two sizes too big. There are eight women including her.

None of them speak about the loss that brings them together, but Elsa knows everyone knows about hers. It's the kind of tragedy that travels well. The slow, torturous ones are easier to keep private. Less gossip worthy. The group leader, Bethany, orbits the other women as they butter and cream and sugar. Bethany touches each on the part of the back most like a wing. While the moist heat of her palm permeates the fabric of their colorless blouses and cardigans, she asks, *On a scale of one to ten, ten being the worst, how's your grief today?* As expected, they are fives and sixes. The ones and twos don't group any longer and the nines and tens suffocate in their own private suffering.

After each woman shares their numbers, Autumn, the youngest in the group stands. Her body sways, palms pressed against her low back. The woman looks toward the kitchen for Jordan then sees him with a shovel and bucket in the yard. She's only known Autumn for a few weeks, and is shocked she hadn't before noticed how ugly she is. The fleshy hump of her nose, the tiny dot eyes, the flat path from chin to throat. Her hair is possibly the only thing about her that could be considered attractive with its thick, shiny, hay-shaded coils.

I'm going to have a baby, Autumn says. Her palms slide forward and rest on her stomach. She slides her eyes from woman to woman, perhaps waiting for one to invite her to linger, to offer something other than pity or disgust, to say how wonderful, to say they're sure everything will be alright.

It's not recommended, Bethany says, more to the group than Autumn. Bethany lifts the plate with the scones and passes it to her right. The plate completes the circle as heavy as it began and she sends it on a second round. *Too soon.*

Autumn smiles and her upper lip is lost. She shrugs slightly, almost more like a tick, sits and takes a scone when the plate reaches her. The scone does what scones do when she bites into it but she doesn't bother to sweep away the crumbs from her blouse. Bethany asks the group which of the calming techniques they've tried since the last meeting and to share their degree of effectiveness.

Eventually, Bethany distributes pieces of lined paper and asks them to take their time describing the image that most haunts them today. Each week's meeting closes in this way. Fifteen minutes pass without anyone reaching for their coffee or a scone. Aside from the dog's occasional bark, the only sounds are those of pens scratching image into language. Bethany collects their writing, asks them to think about how their fears differ today than from previous meetings, again pressing her palm to each woman's shoulder. *This is how we heal.*

After the last group member leaves, Elsa hurries to the bathroom. She's barely seated when the diarrhea explodes into the toilet. The sounds her body makes are ridiculous and dramatic, like what you might hear in a movie set in a frat house. She hears the screen door's croak and click then the hush of Jordan's socked feet on the hardwood. The air in the bathroom is thick with the scent of shit but she's afraid to stand to open the window and make a mess. Another round of diarrhea splatters into the toilet.

Okay in there? His voice close enough she knows he can smell her waste.

Something didn't sit well. The scones, I guess. Can I just have some space, please?

He retreats, and she hears the clinking of stacked plates and coffee cups.

Jesus Christ, leave it! I'll clean it up! She's never yelled at him before and the effort raws her throat. She hears him sets down the dishes and the light thud of ascending stairs.

Before the bull had blown through the fence around the backyard, Elsa'd held her son on her shoulders until his weight grieved the muscles in her neck and she'd lifted him and set him on the ground. They stood in their in their red, white, and blue, watching the fireworks. Her son was so awed by the splattering of color in the sky that he hadn't heard her call him back when he bolted toward the fence. The neighbor later admitted he'd set off a dozen M-80s, one after another, and that it was likely the constant sound of disaster that had sent the bull on his final charge. Elsa was promised it had happened quickly—the clean snap of the neck and severing of the spinal cord—they promised her son had felt no pain.

When the rage in her gut finally calms, she leaves the bathroom. As instructed, Jordan has left the dishes in the sink for her. She pulls on the rubber gloves, squirts in the soap and fills the sink with hot water. Through the window above the kitchen sink she sees the dog asleep in the grass. Everything is only green and brown. The swing sways because the breeze refuses to let it be. Somewhere, disaster is just a tick away, and people are failing to enjoy the final seconds of its before.

Brine and Bone

Every Saturday since the crash, we barefooted the barnacled rocks that had snagged the proof of others. We waited for the tide to shore our mother or the sky to earth her. It was my sister Eleanor's job to lift the rocks, and she squatted, feet spread wide as her hips. When she reached out, her sleeves shifted to reveal wrists red and raw with scratch, and though I couldn't see her palms from where I stood, I knew there were blisters, some new and pink and puffed with fluid, some already flattened from the burst.

The silt released the rock with a slurp, and its underneath scattered. We'd once spent hours collecting crabs on this beach, clasping them like our father had shown us to avoid the pinch, then flipping them belly up hoping to see the mass of eggs. I now let them scatter untouched. The once shunned blips of slick sea worms burrowed without insult, and the tiny dartfish, once thought the ultimate find, pierced the water without interruption. We weren't there to delight in the complexity of lives we believed were so simple. We were looking for anything of her. And every week we found nothing.

Our father joined us for the first month. He wore a backpack so full of things for us it rawed the skin on his shoulders. We were old enough to pack for ourselves, but he did it anyway. Water bottles, apple and cheese slices, granola bars, sunscreen. He brought honey for my cough, and Eleanor's ankle brace in case of uneven rocks. We were six and two to him, and I had to push back when he squirted sunscreen into his palm and asked me to stand still.

Hours into our first Saturday, he spread out a water-proof blanket on the sand and set out our snacks. He sliced the apples so thin they dissolved on my tongue. He'd put our food in containers with multiple compartments to keep everything from each other. We hadn't used them for food in years.

We stared at the bay while we ate, and I tried to think of something to say that wasn't about how I felt. I was a hundred feet from the bay, my legs soggy with brine. My father asked me something and the answer sent me into a coughing fit. He dug through the bag and handed me the honey then sat on a beach log behind my sister to French braid her hair. He'd never done it before, but that morning I'd seen him watching a How-To video. His starter strands were too thick and I knew the braid would fail, but I swallowed the honey, kept my mouth shut.

Dozens of searchers scattered the shore, doing exactly what we were doing. I recognized some of them from the press conferences and support group. Most of the people had lost fathers and husbands on their way to meetings and conferences and though everyone seemed sure their loss was the worst, only a few were right. One man scrambled along the boulders, too far from the shore to find anything, I thought, looking for something left of his wife and three daughters. There was no logic to where he searched, but even less so as to why he didn't walk into the bay and take a deep breath.

Eleanor squawked when the brush snagged and my father tugged it free. He shush-shushed her and started another braid. I grabbed two cheese slices even though they would give me a stomachache. After we ate, my father designated patches of the shore for each of us. Before we scattered, he made us promise to call him close if we found something and not to touch it, no matter how hard it was to resist.

I took my sandwich to my assigned patch, which was more tide pool than rock or sand, and unlikely anything could wash up and over and into. I was fine with this. Finding would be worse than not finding. We were assured by now any biological remains washing up unlikely, but that wasn't the only thing of her that could destroy.

I sat on a rock and ate my sandwich. Just under the surface, barnacles fanned their feathery legs to catch the food too tiny to see. My father had made peanut butter and jelly sandwiches, which I hadn't had for years, and I wondered why I'd ever stopped eating them. My sister crouched in her assigned patch, and I watched her start the lift and lower of rocks. When she reached forward, a strip of skin above her waist band exposed tracks the color of raspberries her fingernails had carved.

What I thought was a fit of seagulls was actually a woman down shore, clutching something to her chest while a man wrapped his arms around her. I waited for her to drop to her knees like I'd seen others do when they'd found something, as though being closer to the earth eased the ache, but she remained standing, only hunched by the weight of the man. I couldn't tell what she was holding, maybe a piece of a blouse or jacket, maybe a patch of carpet or seat. Maybe it was just something that once belonged to the sea, but she saw what she needed to.

I felt a flutter then a seagull tore the sandwich from my hand. It got the whole thing, and disassembled it as it flew off. I waited for my father to rage at me or the seagull, but his eyes were on the woman. A man in a yellow jacket approached her with a plastic bag. I couldn't hear what they were saying, but the woman's hands flailed with the disaster of useless language until she dropped it into the bag. Whatever it was looked small enough to be nothing from where I stood. When I looked back toward my father our things were packed, the blanked folded. Nobody said anything when we left, but we all had a feeling he wouldn't join us again.

Each week, something of others continued to be found. An *East of Eden* paperback. A flip flop, foam pressed dark into the print of a single, unique footprint. A bottle of medicated shampoo. Lipstick in Chatterbox Pink. A paddle hair brush. Box of tampons in a Ziploc bag.

Each finding hunched us. Though my father didn't come, he continued to pack us lunches, water, and sunscreen and always asked to braid my sister's hair before we left. She always let him.

When Eleanor asked every Friday if we were going to search, I said yes, because I needed to feel like I was of any use at all to her, but I'd given up. Items were still being recovered, but everything looked like it belonged to my mother, or nothing did. I realized how little I paid attention to her things. It was getting more difficult for me to breathe, especially on the shore where the humidity was high. I'd told the doctor it felt like there was water at the bottom of my lungs, too far down for the cough to reach. She said everyone had their own way of grieving and prescribed me an inhaler.

The doctor was right, of course. My sister's grief had made her grow two inches in eight weeks. Impossible, of course, but it happened. The hem of her pants refused to cover the tops of her socks and flip flops were the only shoes that fit. If my father noticed, he didn't say or do anything. He'd always been careful not to mention anything about the changing shape and size of our bodies. I knew mine was doing its own thing too. There was a constant ache in my stomach like I needed to eat so I did as much as I could. Even still, my pants wouldn't stop slipping off my hips, and I found my sister's fit me right.

By the eighth Saturday, the crowd of searchers had thinned to the man who'd lost his wife and daughters, a woman who was now clearly pregnant searching for her husband, and us. I'm not sure if everyone else had found something or had given up. For the first couple weeks, Christ the King church members had set up a table with coffee, hot chocolate and cookies for searchers, but they'd since moved onto another disaster.

Eleanor continued to be the rock lifter and offered to do it for the pregnant woman. I lay the blanket out and got out what my father had packed. When he first sent us on our own, the food he packed had been indulgences—chips, donuts, soda, fruit leather—but today he'd packed blueberries, cheese cubes, cherry tomatoes and cashews. I ate all the cheese while my sister chatted with the pregnant woman and put her hand on her arm with a "let me lift it for you."

The man with the lost wife and children approached and asked to sit on the blanket. He sat and set out a bag of beef jerky. I took a piece and it kept my mouth busy so I didn't say anything, and neither did he. It was the first Saturday of fall, and the sky was the color of dishwater. I looked at my sister and tried to squint away the haze that seemed to follow me everywhere. I noticed for the first time the peaks of her breasts.

My father's braiding had improved considerably and he'd managed two today, tight from the top to the tips. My sister had suddenly become beautiful. The man held out the packet of jerky and I took another piece even though I'd only gummed the first. My cough had finally gone away, but my lungs still felt thick and wet and I'd started hiccupping. We ate jerky and watched my sister lift and lower rocks for a lifetime.

Finally, she came to me and said it was time to go. When I stood, my legs felt as useless as fins, and my feet barely left a print on the sand. She offered me her arm, and I saw her wrist was smooth, the color of the rest of her skin. Though my father had told us not to tell anyone, I considered telling the man we hadn't known our mother was on the plane until my father got a phone call after the crash.

The last morning with her, our mother made us scrambled eggs and toast, reminded Eleanor about the puppy sitting she was doing for our neighbor, asked me when I thought I'd be home that night. I wanted to ask the man why he wasn't with his family on that plane. I wanted to ask him what kind of father lets his children blow into a million pieces. I wanted to ask him what it was like to know they died terrified, waiting for their terrified mother to say it would be okay. I wanted to ask how he can open his eyes in the morning and bother with the inhale. I knew there was suffering worse than mine, and I wanted to feel it.

My sister motioned to me, so I gathered my things slowly because that was how my hands moved. I could tell by her movements she was asking the pregnant woman questions and the pregnant woman was answering them. She pointed at the ocean, which was as flat as saran wrap and the color of coal. The man was on our blanket, but his gaze was lost in the ghosted ocean so we left it with him.

Our father was waiting for us in the parking lot. My sister got in the front seat and I didn't complain. I sat in the middle and tightened the seatbelt. My father asked how it had gone, and when my hiccups flared, I let my sister answer. Her voice flooded my ears. She chatted about the pregnant woman who was only six weeks from her due date and had invited Eleanor to her baby shower. Mermaids were the theme. I couldn't stop blinking to clear away the fog.

Eleanor was my mother's favorite, but I loved my mother more than she did. I didn't blame her—Eleanor was simply a more pleasant person than I was. She had a light about her people often said. At a restaurant one night, a woman had taken my mother aside and complimented her on her beautiful children. She then motioned toward Eleanor and said "She's a direct line to God." I never forgot that moment, how my cheeks had pinked at not being good enough, how ashamed I felt when my mother took my sticky hand and said "I know."

Though he'd driven us each Saturday for two months, my father made a trip that should have taken an hour last two. I wrapped myself in his coat and thought about trying to sleep before the hiccups came back. My fingertips were full of the throb of nails chewed too short, though I'd never been a nail biter. There were too many roadside crosses to count, ones that had nothing to do with me or the plane crash. I tried to catch the carved names and dates, but things were mostly dark smudges. Sometimes I saw letters, but couldn't make out the words they made.

The following Saturday was the same: me, Eleanor, the pregnant woman (who my sister had started calling Sarah) and the man who'd lost the most. My father had taken Eleanor shopping for school and didn't complain when she got into the car wearing a new outfit. She'd started wearing make-up, too, or had she for a while? There were a few years when I was the prettier one, at least on the outside, but now my eyes looked like coal pressed deep into dough, and a downy fuzz had appeared on my face and arms. I thought about how the doctor said everyone grieves differently, and at least the cough and hiccups were gone.

The man was already sitting on our blanket when we got there. My legs didn't want to work right, so I crawled toward it. My sister already had her palms pressed to Sarah's stomach by the time I got there. The man didn't say mention the crawling or anything else. Though there were no more coughs or hiccups, I'd been burping a lot, each dislodging a warm gush of fluid I swallowed without tasting. The man held the beef jerky out and I took a piece even though I knew I couldn't eat. The wind picked up a scent, and I saw a dark continent of urine on my jeans.

The shore refused the tug of the tide. The ocean gave back what it didn't want or need, but we'd found nothing of our mother. Though we hadn't admitted it, we couldn't deny she had been leaving us. Why wouldn't she? What had we ever done not to deserve being left? What had we ever done other than need, than want? I searched for some damage to settle into, some pocket of raging muscle or stormy gut, but I felt nothing but a pulse. I looked at the man.

I knew from the news his daughters were two, five, and eight. Hazel, Harper, and Emma: names they'd probably chosen because they would be good to grow into. I knew there was enough time for the passengers to realize the disaster they were about to become a part of. For our mother to realize she was about to destroy us. I wondered if she wished we were with her at that moment, about to burst into a billion pieces a mile high more than she wished she was earthed. Maybe she fastened her own breathing device then moved onto Hazel's for a last chance at acting like a mother. Maybe she shushed her screams, promised everything was going to be fine—it was just a storm they had to pass through.

I reached toward someone but nothing moved. My eyes were full of gray sky, lungs flat with the bottom of a breath. Some time passed, I think, before I felt the sensation of being lifted, the inconsistent motion of an uneven path, the resistance of the ocean's surface before its acceptance. The water chilled my body until I felt no difference between salt and skin, mineral and muscle, brine and bone.

With Gratitude

Thank you to the editors who've supported my work and their tireless efforts to create safe and enlightening literary spaces. Thank you to the writers and professors whose words and encouragement have inspired, awed, and illuminated, especially Ramona Ausubel, Rebecca Brown, Carol Guess, Kimberly King Parsons, and Kathryn Trueblood.

Thank you to Unsolicited Press for their encouragement, trust, and patience.

Thank you to my creative writing students at Western Washington University for their grace, compassion, and kindness toward me and their peers, especially over the past two years.

Thank you to my literary inner circle: Cynthia Hollenbeck, Kelly Magee, and Elizabeth Vignali, whose careful, honest, and constructive feedback over the last two decades has been as unwavering as their friendship.

Thank you to Michael for the gift of space and time to write, and unconditional loyalty and love. To Scarlet and Evelyn, whose creativity, empathy, and commitment to equity encourages me every day to be better. To my family, immediate and extended, and friends from all factions of my life, who never fail to show up and cheer me on.

About the Author

Kami Westhoff's work has appeared or is forthcoming in various journals including *Meridian, Carve, Third Coast, The Pinch, Decomp, Eclectica, Waxwing, Passages North, Redivider,* and *West Branch.* Her chapbook, *Sleepwalker,* won the 2016 Dare to Be Chapbook Contest from Minerva Rising Press. Her poetry collection, cowritten with Elizabeth Vignali, *Your Body a Bullet* was released by Unsolicited Press in 2018. She teaches Creative Writing at Western Washington University in Bellingham, WA.